William Lawrence

Life of Amos A. Lawrence

With extracts from his diary and correspondence

William Lawrence

Life of Amos A. Lawrence
With extracts from his diary and correspondence

ISBN/EAN: 9783337011666

Printed in Europe, USA, Canada, Australia, Japan

Cover: Foto ©Raphael Reischuk / pixelio.de

More available books at **www.hansebooks.com**

LIFE OF
AMOS A. LAWRENCE

WITH EXTRACTS FROM HIS DIARY AND CORRESPONDENCE

BY HIS SON

WILLIAM LAWRENCE

BOSTON AND NEW YORK
HOUGHTON, MIFFLIN AND COMPANY
The Riverside Press, Cambridge
1888

The Riverside Press, Cambridge:
Electrotyped and Printed by H. O. Houghton & Co.

To

MY MOTHER

I Inscribe

THIS VOLUME

PREFACE.

In gathering together these fragments of my father's journal and letters, I have hoped to recall to his family and friends his character and presence.

At the same time I have had another object in view.

Living as he did in the stirring times before and during the war and taking his part in the patriotic, social, commercial, and religious activities, his experience has its practical bearings and his example a close touch upon the life of every man who, like him, wishes to do his simple duty as a citizen. The record of his motives and work may, therefore, have an interest and inspiration which some may not find in the biographies of greater men.

For assistance in this work I am indebted
to a number of his friends, to the Diary and
Correspondence of Amos Lawrence, and especially to Professor L. W. Spring and his
History of Kansas.

W. L.

Cambridge, *January*, 1888.

CONTENTS.

CONTENTS.

CHAPTER IX.

1856–1861.

CHAPTER X.

1861–1862.

CHAPTER XI.

1862–1865.

CHAPTER XII.

CHAPTER XIII.

CHAPTER XIV.

1867–1882.

CHAPTER XV.

1882–1886.

AMOS A. LAWRENCE.

I.

BOYHOOD.

1814–1831.

On the morning of the 19th of April, 1775, Susanna Parker, who lived with her parents on the turnpike in Concord, caught sight of the British troops marching out from Boston, and running with her sister over the hill behind the house watched the gleaming of the muskets along the road. When the soldiers came back that afternoon, pursued by minute men and farmers, the girls again took refuge behind the hill, and on their return to the house found lying dead at the gate a handsome British soldier in his red coat.

That same morning Colonel Prescott rode to the house of his neighbor, Samuel Lawrence, in Groton, and cried out, "Samuel,

notify your men; the British are coming."
Mounting the colonel's horse, Corporal Lawrence rode seven miles, rousing the minute men of his circuit, and was back again
in forty minutes. In three hours the company was ready to march, and on the next
day it reached Cambridge.

At Bunker Hill, Samuel Lawrence received through his beaver hat a musket
ball which cut his hair from front to rear,
and was struck by a spent grape-shot upon
his arm. After serving two years near
Boston and in New York, he returned to
marry Susanna Parker, to whom he had
been engaged since early in 1775. But
during the ceremony the signal was given
to call all soldiers to their posts, and within
an hour he left his bride to join his regiment at Cambridge.

At the close of the war Major Samuel
Lawrence and his wife settled down at the
Lawrence homestead in Groton. He attended to his duties as farmer, deacon, justice of the peace, and trustee of the Academy of which he was a founder, while she
cared for the house and a family of six sons
and three daughters.

In 1807, the fourth son, Amos, with

twenty dollars in his pocket, drove in his father's chaise to Boston and entered business.

In a few years he and his younger brother Abbott founded the house of A. & A. Lawrence, which with a few other leading firms in Boston carried on her foreign commerce, developed the manufactures of Massachusetts, and gave to that generation of Boston merchants a wide reputation for integrity and success.

Amos, who was for many years an invalid, gradually surrendered the active business to the younger members of the firm and devoted himself to philanthropic and public interests, while his sleigh, covered with boys and filled with books and clothing for the poor, was known by every one in town.

Abbott, a man of fine physique and great activity, was the leading member of the firm, an influential representative in Congress, and a successful minister at the Court of St. James.

The three other brothers, Luther, William, and Samuel, rose also to positions of large responsibility in business and civic life; so that when a manufacturing town rose on the banks of the Merrimac below Lowell, it was given by vote of the citizens the name of " Lawrence."

In 1811 Amos Lawrence married Sarah Richards, the daughter of Giles Richards, a man of great ingenuity and of little financial wisdom.

July 31, 1814, their second son was born, and given the name of his maternal grandfather, Amos Adams, who during the Revolution was the minister of the First Church in Roxbury. The mother lived long enough to leave with her two boys and daughter the memory of a sweet and lovely character; and at four years of age Amos was sent, a motherless boy, to the care of his grandmother and aunt Eliza, at the old homestead in Groton.

In this town the descendants of John Lawrence of Wisset, county of Suffolk, England, had lived for several generations as farmers, soldiers, and leading citizens. The associations and picturesque surroundings of the place entered into the constitution of the growing boy and gave him a love for the scenery and farming life of New England.

When on a visit to the homestead in his college days, he wrote: " Groton is a beautiful place, but in particular the old mansion farm exceeds almost any farming scenery I ever saw, excepting the valley of the Connecticut. The house is west of the village a mile, and the farm extends a mile farther west to the Nashua. The slope to the river is gentle, but enough to give a beautiful view of the country for many miles from the high land by the house. The house is not large, a real farmer's house of the best sort; that is, it is painted white, has green blinds, a front yard and a large old elm in front, and a front and two side doors. The barn is larger than the house, probably the best barn in the country, and well stocked always. The other buildings are arranged round the large yard at the side of the house, and just above is a pretty raised ground covered with apple-trees. They make 'lots of cider' and gather good crops. The cattle always look fat and happy, and all is quiet and contentment. My old grandmother lives here still, and I hope will many years to come, if she does not prefer death to old age. My aunt [Mary] is a very pious woman, 'fiery hot' as the country people call her, very Calvinistic in her faith and practice. But besides (and better), she is 'smart,' and knows well how to manage the homestead affairs. She finishes a great part of her work in the forenoon, and in the afternoon, knits, sews, reads, and attends some 'inquiry,' Bible class, or missionary meeting. A great deal of her money does she give to the poor heathen, and a great deal to poor Orthodox students. She is short in stature, brisk, and has a good face, but, peace be with her, she reads her Bible and is consistent with her belief."

On the second marriage of his father in 1821, Amos was brought back to Boston and sent to school in the basement of the First Church in Chauncy Place, on the same site that fifty years later was occupied by his counting-room and warehouse. For a year or two he was taught by Mr. William Wells in the rear of Trinity Church, Summer Street, and at thirteen years of age was sent to a private boarding-school in the North Parish, Andover, which in the fashion of those days was advertised under the ambitious title of " Franklin Academy."

The boys in the boarding-schools of to-day little know what they have escaped by being born in the present generation. Master Putnam of Franklin Academy, famil-iarly called " Old Put " or " Old Hickory," represented a system of education which is more interesting in retrospect than in the realization.

After a few days at the school, Amos wrote to his father : " Mr. Putnam is subject to very bad headaches, which make him very cross and angry : he scolds his wife and makes her cry, and makes the boys walk Spanish if they don't keep out of his way : he hit his son such a clip the other day that he was lame for a week. I never saw a set of boys that minded the master so well before. I find Mr. Putnam is very unsteady in his punishments, and more so, I should think, than a school-master ought to be, as he will beg a boy's pardon after using him badly when he finds he is going to write home." After this, we are not surprised that he adds, " I find a great deal of difficulty in not knowing the laws of the school," while an " N. B." at the end of the letter informs his parent that the under master " Mr. Pierce grows pretty strict now and gave me a pretty good wrench of my ear and hair."

He soon grows less respectful in his references to the master, and speaks of " old Put in old Hickory style, with heavy tread, lowered eyebrows and frequent hems, entering

the school-room," and incidentally mentions
" having some trouble with Mr. Hickory on
Saturday, but he was finally cooled and be-
haved well."

The trouble did not end on Saturday, however, for "a great many little items which
plagued him and occasioned his having a
great many tasks," and " eleven hours of
study a day," and especially his hatred of
Algebra as taught in Franklin Academy,
drove young Amos, who was, as his fellow-
pupils testify, a boy " whose self-respect was
great," to seek his freedom in the woods of
Andover and on the road to New Hampshire.
In a day or two he was brought back, and
after an humble apology to his father and
the master he set about the arduous duty of
obeying his father's request " to observe a
strict conformity to the rules of the school."

However, Mrs. Putnam and the fat kitchen-
girl tempered the school with mercy and
condoled with the boys in trouble. And the
resources which served him through life, riding on horseback, skating, the enjoyment of
the beauties of nature, and an acute interest
in people of all sorts, came to his aid in Andover. These probably did as much towards
the development of his character as the study

of Euclid, the daily task of twenty pages of the Greek Testament, or the worship in the village church, where the singing was led by Captain Osgood at the "big viol," and the sermons were preached by "Rev. Bailey Loring, a just man and a Unitarian so called." Occasional allusions to mugs of sour cider, and the decanters at Jim Stevens' tavern, suggest that Master Putnam's "Tracts on Temperance" were needed at the school; and in answer to a letter which he rather irreverently called a "Temperance Essay" from his father, Amos wrote, "To please you more than to allay any fear of mine, I will consent not to taste a drop of distilled spirit for two years; then, if you wish, I will add four."

The testimony of his school-mates sketch him as an active, "observing, and thoughtful boy, always affable, inviting implicit confidence in his good judgment and honesty of purpose, full of self-respect and respect for others," while letters and diary emphasize a pure-minded, restless lad, with a keen interest in the affairs of the world, and with maturity of thought as to the meaning and purposes of life. The boyish resolutions written before the sunrise of his last New

Year's day at school in 1831, suggest the spirit of his life : " to adhere to veracity, to use as much as in me lies pure and well spoken language, to keep a strict guard against vice and to cherish virtue, to talk sense or not at all."

II.

COLLEGE.

1831–1835.

IN 1831 Amos entered Harvard College without conditions, donned the " University dress " then required of all students, — " the coat of black, single breasted, with a rolling cape square at the end, waist reaching to the natural waist; " and, to quote from a classmate, he was soon " out on the Delta kicking football, full of laughter, and in a state of perpetual motion."

" A man may be honest, active, brave, moral, and religious, and still no scholar," is the true but dangerous text with which the diary of his college life opens.

In the spring term of the Freshman year there occurred one of those little episodes in which the students of a former generation sometimes indulged, namely, a gunpowder plot, followed by an explosion, " the refrageration of divers windows and the demolition

of much movable stuff," a class rebellion, in-
dictments before the grand jury, confession
of the ringleaders, and a number of expul-
sions, suspensions, and letters of advice to
pass a few months in some quiet country
town. Unfortunately Amos had lately
bought some gunpowder for shooting, which
he kept in his room. The plotters thought
that stealing his powder was safer and
cheaper than buying their own; therefore,
on the testimony of the shopkeeper, he was
drawn into the investigation. He was, however, acquitted of all guilt; but the excited
condition of the students made it advisable
for the more restless spirits to rusticate for
a few months.

There soon followed a letter from President Quincy to his father, who was at that
time recovering from a dangerous illness.
"I entirely concur in your wishes to keep
your son from ' every appearance of evil,'
and under all circumstances I have thought
it best to advise to take him away a short
time, say until next commencement, and let
him study under some fellow master. Your
son has not been detected in any connection with the disorders in the hall or in the
chapel. Still, he is young, very susceptible,

and if in a thoughtless moment he should get into any difficulty, in your state of mind and health, it might be injurious; perhaps more than you can bear. I think also the obligation to study, which an instructor, particularly attentive to him, might impose, would be very useful to his future habits."

The result justified President Quincy's wisdom and knowledge of the young man's character. With Mr. John F. Stearns of Bedford, a young Harvard graduate, as his tutor, Amos lived first at Bedford and then in the Mansion House on Andover Hill. Freed for the first time from chafing rules, he developed such a sense of responsibility, and such diligence in study, that from his own choice he prolonged his rustication from six to eighteen months.

Always impatient at listless work, the school methods of study had irritated and disgusted him, and the following extract from his diary at this time is a leaf from his own experience : —

"There is a method of study adopted by many that is highly injurious to mind and body, indeed it is worse than idleness: to sit down with books open, and the mind as un-tutored as the winds, to get a lesson ; to think of the lesson one moment, of the girls one more, and of home one more; then two more of the lesson, and so to spend a day in a shameful waste of time. The body grows crabbed and crooked, and the mind grows empty and weak, and the whole man is destroyed by it. The habit may be contracted at school by boys, where they are obliged to remain a certain number of hours pent up in a room, not allowed to talk or look anywhere except on their books. If Mr. Putnam had compelled his boys to study five hours instead of leaning on their elbows eleven, he would so have habituated them to study that they would not have become such dunces as they are now."

Sometimes the intense moral earnestness of his father's letters chafed him, and his filial respect was tinged with a little pleasantry when, on receipt of an unusually long letter of advice, he answered: "The morality and general observations of your letters, disconnected from the other matters and printed, would make a very instructive volume. When you compel us to shift for ourselves I think we may make a very good beginning by publishing a few copies of your miscellaneous works, and so benefit our neighbors and replenish our pockets at the same time." "Your good advice has the advantage of your bills of exchange, inasmuch as it is current everywhere; if it could only be *cashed*, how fortunate we should be, and how soon we should spoil."

During these months he was again thrown into the scenery which he so much enjoyed. "What a vast space a man leaves empty who does not cultivate a taste for natural beauties," he then wrote. And though the old horse "appellated Doctor White" had "a back formed to shed the rain or to cut the air," yet "it was a pleasure to ride him."

The study of the village characters and his interest in the town meetings, with their lively Orthodox and Liberal discussions, gave him that experience in affairs and that tact in meeting men of all classes which he felt was a part of the education of every American boy, and which served him well in later years.

His practical sense was offended by the raising of a new meeting-house in Bedford; for then, as he wrote, "we shall have three ministers (Orthodox, Unitarian, and Universalist) for 690 inhabitants, 670 of whom

have only the necessaries of life by hard labor. There are only 120 voters, of whom
50 are tipplers, journeymen, shoemakers,
heathen, etc. They can hardly support one
minister, and sixteen would not convert
them."

Theological discussion was rife, and a
young man of Unitarian education, thrown
into the thick of the enemy's ranks at Andover, was naturally set to thinking. For
in those days, as he wrote to his father,
"truth in Cambridge becomes a lie in Andover, and the same of Andover truth when
carried to Cambridge."

Though it is hardly worth the while to
follow him through the arguments by which,
in a strong Andover atmosphere, he was
led to record the fact, "I do not believe
the Unitarian doctrine," yet it is suggestive
of his independence and his dissatisfaction
with both systems, that in Andover he first
bought and studied the Book of Common
Prayer.

Other rusticated students found their way
to Andover. "There is," he writes, "one
who does nothing but smoke and eat. The
divines smoke and eat too, but in subor-

dination to more important considerations; a good argument, for instance, is more relished than all the puddings for a term." Still the solemnity of the theological students oppressed him, his tutor's health had begun to fail for want of something to laugh at, and he begged his father "to send up one or two comic almanacs to lend to the students as an act of charity." The life there led him to consider the question, "Which is the worst crime, intemperance in study or in drinking? Both of them tend to shorten life and to embitter it; both are suicides."

An occasional ride to Groton and other towns varied the monotony. He attended a Concord celebration, where "Mr. Hopkinson exerted himself to the uttermost. His delivery was Cambridge precisely, and that is almost no delivery at all." But the great event was the visit of President Jackson, which he thus described : —

" I went to Boston to see President Jackson, who, with his Cabinet, has been making a triumphal tour, as it were, of the Northern States. The Bostonians honored him as much as he deserves, perhaps more. I saw the old gentleman first in a procession near

the State House.   His appearance struck
me instantly with a kind of respect for him,
it is so remarkable.   He alone was uncov-
ered, and displayed a head higher than those
about him, and silvered with age.   His hair
is remarkable on account of its thickness,
and his fashion of combing it back.   He re-
viewed the troops and showed himself an
accomplished horseman.   From Boston he
went to Salem, thence to Lowell through
Andover.   I was one of the cavalcade here
and had a very good sight of him.   He put
up at this house and ate a lunch of bread
and milk in his chamber.   Mr. Van Buren,
Vice-President, dined in Mr. Skinner's parlor, and so did Major Donelson and myself,
and some other of the illustrious.   We es-
corted him out of town, took a stage coach
and followed him to Lowell, where we arrived just in time to see the famous procession of factory girls.   It consisted of three
or four thousand, marching by fours.   This,
if nothing else, was a splendid sight for the
old general."

In the spring vacation of 1834, following
his return to college, Mr. Lawrence, with his
tutor, Henry R. Cleveland, and his classmate,
Charles H. Gates, made a visit to Washington.

Just before reaching Philadelphia they experienced for the first time the wonderful sensation of riding in a steam carriage, but the new invention did not seem to have brought civilization into the filthy streets of the Quaker city, in which a great number of " grunters " luxuriated. In Washington he found that the far-famed David Crockett reigned in the lobby; that " Clay pestered Van Buren and then took two or three pinches of snuff from the Vice-President's snuff-box; " that Van Buren was " a great gallant for one so small and old too."

He was in the House when Mr. Adams presented a petition for the abolition of slavery in the District of Columbia. " At this," he wrote, " every Southern member took fire; the most absurd resolutions were introduced, denouncing Mr. Adams as an agitator, an incendiary, and as offering gross insult to the House and to the feelings of the members of the South, in presenting such a petition. One resolution was to expel Mr. Adams, another was to burn his petition, and another to arraign him before the bar of the House." " If there ever was an eloquent speaker and an able debater, a good theoretical philosopher, it is he. I never heard such argument expressed so eloquently before, and never expect to again. He covered his opponents with ridicule, and excited the laughter of the House; the effect you see in the vote and resolutions."

Of course Mr. Webster filled the eye of a Massachusetts young man. "After Mr. Calhoun's second speech, Mr. Webster rose, and the effect was wonderful. His eloquence is appreciated because he seldom nowadays makes an exhibition of it. The members of the other House were crowded around the President's chair, and the Senators' seats and the galleries were full. But when Mr. Webster stood up, all was as still as though the hall was empty. He merely made a motion to adjourn till Monday, which had been made before by Mr. Buchanan."

But the two features of Washington to the college student were Gadsby's Hotel and President Jackson.

"Gadsby's Hotel is an immense building as large as a small town, so that the dinner-bell is in a belfry on the top, like that of a church. When this sounds, the crowds of boarders — a motley mass, collected from every State in the Union, and Christendom, we might say — move in an irresistible tide toward the hall, and seat themselves every one in his chair, while clouds of black servants stand behind in mute array. All look about to see who is there, and try to smell what lies hid under the covers. They snuff and rub their hands, take a drink of brandy and water, which is always on the table, and wait the word of command: the negroes' eyes twinkle for the same, and all of them wait impatiently for it, eying old Gadsby like eagles. He stands at the head of the board (an elderly, short, white-headed man), and when he sees his legions ready and all still, he braces up his shoulders, looks at the whole, and then at the waiters, opens his mouth, and raises his hand, then says 'Uncover!' Then is the time to stop your ears, for every blacky leaps at all the covers within his reach, up they raise them with a stupendous flourish, and the air seems made of silver; but look out and not turn your head too much, or the consequences may be fatal."

"Our friend Mr. Franklin Pierce very kindly offered to carry us to see President Jackson."

"It was his business hour, and we only expected him to shake hands with us, and per-

mit us to look through his halls. We
looked at his tobacco pipe and about the
room till all was clear, and then Mr. Pierce
opened the door and asked leave to intro-
duce us. With that the gentleman arose,
met us at the door and shook hands with
us very cordially, and asked us to sit down,
which we did and looked at him from head
to foot, surprised to find ourselves so suddenly in the presence of the great cause of
so much dispute, honest and dishonest, that
has divided this whole country. Here sat
the grand mover of the machine that sup-
ports some and crushes others. He ad-
dressed himself almost wholly to Mr. Pierce,
thinking rightly, I suppose, that we came
merely to see him. And, by the way, I for-
got to say that Mr. Pierce, at our request,
introduced us as members of Harvard College. The old man recollected the LL. D.
he received here last year, and the device
took, which accounts, I suppose, in some
measure for the politeness with which he received us. But he is a very polite man, as
everybody who is introduced to him finds,
unless they come on bank business, or something else he hates."

On Mr. Lawrence's return to college his

classmates found him the same fun-loving, active, social man; but his character had deepened and developed. He still chafed at the routine of college studies and kept his mind alert. He read with enthusiasm on subjects which interested him, and also made such studies and records of the characters of his classmates as show him to have reached a deeper sense of the responsibilities of life.

The record of his own future, written early in his senior year, shows that his plans and principles were already formed, for they were carried out in action even to the least detail.

" My present design is to be a merchant, not a plodding, narrow-minded one pent up in a city, with my mind always in my counting-room, but (if there be such a thing possible) I would be at the same time a literary man in some measure and a farmer. That is, I would live in the country a few miles from town (excepting when devoted to business, which would be the forenoons), and there I would read and work on my farm. My advantages for becoming rich are great: if I have mercantile tact enough to carry on the immense though safe machine which my father and uncle have put in operation, it will turn out gold to me as fast as I could wish : and to be rich would be my delight. I consider it an oyster-like dulness, and not a pious or enlightened way of thinking, that makes some despise riches. If any one has any love for his fellow creatures, any love of the worthy respect of his neighborhood, he will be willing and glad to be rich. They say riches are a burden that harass the soul and lead into temptation : so they are to the miser who is in constant fear of losing his acquisitions, and to the profligate who receives an inheritance merely to squander it on his passions. A good man will willingly endure the labor of taking care of his property for the sake of others whom he can so much benefit by it, but his thoughts and fears will not be perpetually on the alert that he may not lose a dollar and may not make all he can. If one can be rich and yet for his private ease will not be, he is almost as loving of himself as he who heaps up only to count his dollars, and refuses the demands of charity."

At last the class of 1835 " all joined hands and danced around the Liberty tree, and in the afternoon they danced still more and drank pails of punch. Then after a supper at Fresh Pond," they separated ; but to the last day of his life, Mr. Lawrence sustained an active interest in every classmate and received great satisfaction from their interest in him.

III.

FIRST YEARS IN BUSINESS.

1835–1839.

A FEW days after Class Day Mr. Lawrence was in Lowell, studying the mills. Soon he took a position with Almy, Patterson & Co., where he could learn the business of a dry-goods commission merchant, for by inheritance and opportunity that seemed to be his future line of work.

In July, 1836, being attacked with varioloid, he was quarantined for several weeks at Rainsford Island. Soon after this, he went, in company with two business friends, on a journey through the West and South, to examine credits for Boston firms just before the financial crisis of 1837, and to make business acquaintances through the country. Travelling by canal through Pennsylvania, they reached Pittsburgh in the height of the Presidential canvass. "Seeing a crowd around the dinner hall," Mr. Lawrence wrote,

"I went in, and found General Harrison making a speech about the abuses of government, his political course, and his designs if elected to the presidential chair. After this I was introduced to him. His right hand was disabled by shaking hands with so many people, but he still continued it notwithstanding the pain it gave him. The operatives were there in their shirtsleeves, unwashed and unshaved, and received great attention, and the boys loitering about the door were sure to be patted when the general came near them."

Ohio was then near the frontier. "The population of Ohio is the most unmannerly I ever saw. There is no elegance, no good breeding in the country towns we have been in; perhaps we ought not expect it. Troops of travellers and farmers come up to the door and dismount, take off their saddlebags, and give their horses to the hostler. They take a glass of toddy and sit down in the bar-room till their dinner is ready, then light a cigar and get on their horses again, and so they jog over the country."

Down the Mississippi they met the border life. " We stopped at a town called Paducah, and I went up to the shops on the bluff to get a pencil and see the town. The stationer's shop was well stocked with pistols, bowie knives, and tobacco; perhaps there were books and paper in the drawers, but for lead pencils there were none except of solid lead covered with red paper, such as measurers of boards and timber use. I bought one, however."

Looking for a church on Sunday in a small Kentucky town, they found a few scholars in a Sunday-school in a log-cabin. "The grog shops were open, and drunkards were lolling about. One or two were lying down in the street. There were two fights in the course of the day, and two fellows were stuck with knives."

He wrote from Georgia, "the want of thrift among the farmers is beyond our comprehension. This must arise from their ignorance of reading and writing, and consequently their want of facility of information. What I had imagined a Southern planter is a very rare sight. I mean a well-educated gentleman."

"We continually meet the caravans of the planters moving into Alabama. First comes a covered cart, drawn by mules and horses, from every corner of which peep the round, woolly heads of a dozen little negroes, all laughing (I believe a negro child never cries), except those who are asleep. After this one or two or three teams with furniture and more negroes, according to the riches of the 'mover.' Behind all, the family ride in their carryall and wagons or on horseback, and the grown negroes hunt squirrels along the woods or straggle along as their inclination leads them. Some of these processions are very ragged, but the negroes are dressed as warm as their masters, and sometimes seem pretty much on an equality with them; and deservedly so, for they know about as much."

In Virginia, the condition was better. "The negroes in the country appear healthy and happy and are always respectful. A planter or any white person passing a negro almost always nods, bids him a good day or inquires for his master, and a negro touches his hat or takes it off, if he is well bred, when he meets a carriage."

On account of his father's retirement from active business, Mr. Lawrence did not have the opportunity for which he had hoped, of entering the office of A. & A. Lawrence & Co., and in time stepping into the position and success which that firm had won. But thrown back upon his own resources, he determined to hew out his own path, and to succeed or fail on his merits as a business man.

Consequently he opened his own counting-room in a corner of the Phillips Building near Liberty Square, and for three years was a commission merchant for broadcloths, cassimeres, and silks. His financial success was all that could be expected in the dull times following the crisis of 1837, but his first object evidently was to know business men and their methods and to gain a good mercantile reputation. That he succeeded in these would seem to be shown by the fact that within two years he was made a director of the Suffolk Bank and a member of the corporation of the Provident Institution for Savings, of which he became a trustee in 1841. Through these and other associations he was thrown in with men of an earlier generation, which from a business view was to his advantage, but in later years tended to make him feel older than he really was.

His life was much like that of any other intelligent young man who moved in the pleasant provincial life of Boston in the last generation. He received at his counting-room the first of that line of beggars which was unbroken for fifty years, he rode his horse, and in the evenings either read, wrote an article for the paper, or joined a cotillon party at some hospitable mansion, where the brass-buttoned blue, olive, or claret coats of the gentlemen added a brilliancy and picturesqueness unknown to the present generation of black dress suits.

With the other young men and women of the day he waxed enthusiastic over the lectures of Ralph Waldo Emerson. "Have heard an enchanting lecture from Mr. Emerson at the Lyceum. It savored very much of Coleridge's doctrine, but was certainly the most beautiful and strong composition I ever listened to." "His mind is of a poetical cast and he likes metaphysics ; his philosophy is admirable and his lectures are made more pleasing by a musical but manly voice and a very graceful delivery." "Have read Ralph Waldo Emerson's oration at Cambridge and delight in it. Reading his writings and, still more, hearing him speak is charming, it enlivens the soul and elevates it beyond all fear." "If his practice is as beautiful as his thoughts, if the nature of his thoughts is always the same, he must live very happily."

In these years Mr. Lawrence had his first taste of public service. His journal records: "I am a fireman; the old department resigned, and we better sort of folks took their place. It was hard work for a few nights, but we have slept quietly now for a week. Fires two mornings in succession at four and six o'clock, long before daylight, down in India Street. I turn out with my engine."

"A bad riot took place on Broad Street on Sunday between the Irish and the workmen, — the Irish beaten, their houses pillaged, property destroyed, and some thirty or forty carried to jail by the Yankees. A military force was put in motion after two or three hours and the confusion ended. I shouldered a musket and joined my company as a volunteer, and was kept on guard all night. William did the same. We ought to have a prompt force to act on the instant. I should like to be one to be drilled and armed and at the command of the mayor in an instant; then these mobs would be down before they should disgrace our city by their violence." Later he adds: "Squad drill. We have a squad of H. W. Dehon, C. H. Parker, T. Dexter, two Murdocks, Ingalls, H. Lee, Ch. Wild, etc. We meet over Faneuil Hall three times a week, and go through a drill under Sergeant Williams of the United States Army. My brother William got it up. I think it a shame for a citizen, a gentleman, not to know military movements enough to use a musket."

At the same time his interest in religion deepened. On Sunday mornings he followed the habits of his father and uncles by attending Brattle Street Church, where Dr. Lothrop preached. In the afternoons his increasing interest in the Episcopal Church led him into St. Paul's, which was then under the ministration of Rev. J. S. Stone, D. D. Occasionally he would go to hear Dr. Channing, of whom he says : " He is diminutive in the pulpit, but his eye and countenance are full of spirit and determination." From this time there occurs in his diary the frequent record of those prayers and religious aspirations which we find in the memoirs of most religious lives, but which lose much of their reality and meaning in cold type.

" Last night of the year 1837.

" I thank my God, who has protected and blessed me and brought me to the close of the year in peace and health. I have misspent a great deal of time and can only make new resolutions for the future, on which I implore Divine favor. Great God, regard me in kindness and illumine my mind with heavenly light that may I distinguish truth from error, and in the pursuit of truth give me perseverance. Save me and my friends from that anguish of mind which accompanies fear. May I not fear any but Thee.

" For Christ's sake pardon my sins, and may I always live so as to be willing to die.

" Extend thy truth to the ends of the world and cause to cease violence and prejudice, and hasten the time when religion shall possess all minds. Grant my prayer for Christ's sake."

In 1832, Mr. Jeremiah Mason, who once divided the leadership of the Portsmouth bar with Daniel Webster, had been induced by his brother-in-law, Mr. Amos Lawrence, to remove to Boston and become his near neighbor. In 1838 the marriage of their children, Susan Lawrence to the Rev. Charles Mason, Rector of St. Peter's Church, Salem, bound the two families by a closer tie, which was strengthened a few years later by the business partnership of the two sons, Robert M. Mason and Mr. Lawrence.

In December, 1838, occurred also the marriage of Mr. Lawrence's only brother, William, to Susan Dana, who, as Amos wrote, " by her simple manners, her good sense, and her personal beauty has won the hearts of all who have seen her."

Through 1839 the business of the country was very unsettled, and the United States Bank suspended specie payment. So Mr. Lawrence decided to take this opportunity to close up his business and to go to Europe. In company with his brother-in-law, Charles Mason, he sailed on November 16, in the " Great Western."

IV.

EUROPE.

1839–1840.

THOSE long, descriptive letters which our fathers wrote from Europe, and which were read in the family circle and passed on to the neighbors, have lost their value as completely as the rejected newspaper articles of the same period. Nevertheless, there was often a personal element in them which shed light on the tastes and interests of the writers. Passing through England, Mr. Lawrence experienced that " feeling of home " which a common blood and language create in every intelligent American.

His method in sight-seeing and his practical sense are suggested in the letters to his father from Rome : —

ROME, *April* 16, 1840.

DEAR FATHER, — . . . In order to have a correct idea of Rome one must refer more to books than is necessary in any other city;

on this account I have spent till twelve
o'clock every day except during the Carnival
in reading, and from that till five o'clock in
visiting everything to which I could obtain
admission.

. . . There are forty or more Americans
here, whom I have not seen often, thinking
it rather a waste of time to spend it in visiting those one sees at home. There are several promising young artists among them
studying their profession, particularly a
young man named Crawford, who has suddenly executed a piece of sculpture of the
highest order almost without tools to work
with. His poverty induced him to make too
great exertions, and when he had completed
his work he was seized with a fever, which
attacked his brain, and came near ending his
life. He is now almost recovered, and very
much encouraged by the praises which are
bestowed on his work. Mr. Greene has
made a subscription paper for money to enable him to execute it in marble, and in the
mean time he has received several orders for
busts, which he executes with great quickness, and transfers to marble with great
beauty. He will soon have the means of
accomplishing his main work, and as soon

as it is finished it will be sent to the United
States for exhibition and sale. The young
man is very pleasing in his appearance, and
is a hard student, so that with his genius for
this art he will sooner or later succeed. . . .
The cause of the poverty of this country is
not that the land is not cultivated, nor that
the people are unwilling to work ; but that,
having become too numerous for the land,
a great proportion must be idle, at least a
part of the time. If mechanic labor were
encouraged, the difficulty would be obviated,
as they could then export the product and
receive an equivalent, and like England
grow rich: but the policy of the government of the Church is so far very bad, and
the encouragement to laboring men to leave
their homes and travel hundreds of miles as
pilgrims, not only not doing themselves any
good, but using the money of the people
through whose territory they pass, the establishment of so many holy days when work
is discouraged, the monopolies which cramp
trade, all lead one to believe that the design
is to make the people dependent by not giving them means of getting rich.

His account of the drive from Rome to

Florence gives a graphic sketch of Italy fifty years ago : —

FLORENCE, *May* 4, 1840.

. . . I never had a more agreeable journey than from Rome, arriving here a week ago, and never was in a more delightful city than this.

" The first day we rode through a fertile country of hill and valley, stopping at Monte Rosa and Nepi, all old fortified towns, to Castellana, where we spent the first night. At sunset I strolled out to see the environs, and the people after they had finished their day's labor. It was a fine sight from the decayed walls to look down five hundred feet to the river winding through a deep ravine, on the other side of which green meadows, covered with luxuriant vegetation, stretch out many miles to the mountains. We follow the green almost to the tops, which are covered with snow. The laborers were returning from the fields to the town in groups, toiling up the ascent to it by narrow winding paths, the women were all in the streets or on the heights waiting for them, and the children were running and crawling in every direction. All were gay, all dirty; one cannot be in bad humor after seeing so much

contentment in so great poverty. A post
carriage with-four horses was passing the
immense stone bridge, and two guards who,
according to the old custom, accompany it,
were riding up the hill. The goatherds
· were driving their goats into the town to be
milked; the bells of the two convents were
ringing; the soldiers of the little garrison
were strolling about, smoking their pipes, or
playing at some game on the parapets; and
the whole scene reminded me of some of the
descriptions given by Mrs. Radcliffe in her
novels; probably it was very much the same
two hundred years ago as now. I turned
into the town again, and hearing music, I
went into the cathedral. There were lights
around the altar, but the rest of the church
was almost dark, and one could not distinguish the faces of those kneeling; a faint
light was sometimes thrown over the grim
effigies which ornament the tombs of the
crusaders and the bishops who died hundreds of years ago, and the old Gothic and
Saracenic architecture could hardly be
traced. After listening to the monotonous
chant of the priests I proceeded toward the
" Albergo Reale," where I was to pass the
night. I had not gone far before I was star-

tled by a loud voice calling to me, "for the love of God, to give help to a poor soul in prison." I looked up and saw just above me a heavy grating, through which an ugly looking fellow had thrust his head; he put his hand out at another opening, and repeated his prayer in a hideous tone, but changed it to a hearty curse when I turned away from him, and the guard, coming up with his musket, stopped his prayers and curses together by a stroke of his bayonet, which forced him to draw his head into his cell again. This is a specimen of what one meets within all the towns: gayety, poverty, devotion, villainy, and soldiery.

Returning through England, he caught a glimpse of the men of that day.

BOSTON, OLD ENGLAND, *August* 1, 1840.

DEAR FATHER, — One day I went upon the floor of the House of Lords, where I was almost among the debaters : Lord Brougham was talking next to me, the chancellor of the exchequer, etc. The Duke of Wellington went fast asleep; he appears quite old and has had several strokes of paralysis, so that the country will probably before long mourn his loss. But he is not any older in his feelings than other men. He comes into the House dressed in white linen pantaloons (in a cold day), a military undress coat, white waistcoat and cravat, with a riding whip in his hand. Like most of the members he keeps his hat on, and sleeps more than any of them. I noticed that he staggers somewhat in his walking, but when he mounts his horse he sits firmly and looks remarkably well, so that if you did not know who he was you would turn to look at him. Lord Melbourne reminds me of Mr. Van Buren. He evidently goes into the House, as they say in college, "on tick;" that is, he has so many things to attend to, loves his ease so well, and has such ready talents, that he trusts to luck and to his wits to get through with the business.

Your affectionate son,

A. A. L.

The misery in Ireland appealed to his tender sympathies, while the temperance crusade of Father Mathew aroused his enthusiasm.

Dear Father, — The country of Ireland is in many parts beautiful, but of the wretchedness and suffering of the people, one who has not seen it can hardly form an idea. To say that they are all ragged would be less than the truth; the disease and almost nakedness seen in this cold climate renders the journey unpleasant, and prevents all enjoyment. To see ragged people is not so bad, after one has been in Italy, as the sight of pale women and children, haggard men, and crippled boys, without any means of living, or even of being sheltered. This is so universal, and the loathsomeness of disease so perpetually thrust before a stranger, that I believe it would be impossible for a woman, or any person of delicate feelings, to travel in some parts where I have been. One is surprised and incensed at the supineness of the English Parliament and people, as well as the Irish nobility and proprietors, in not feeling more for these 7,000,000 of their fellow-beings, and at their love of power, which impels them to hold under taxation a country suffering to such extremity. To be a Radical is natural enough when one sees such an abuse of power, and to hope for a revolution or war which will overthrow this system of government is not unreasonable in the Irish. The police is seen everywhere, and the support of this, with the army, which is distributed through the counties, the Lord Lieutenancy and his court in Dublin, together with the Church of England which is planted everywhere, is enough to drain them to the last drop. This you know all about, but I supposed that the accounts we get might have been exaggerated for political effect, and I am glad to have seen exactly the truth, which cannot be known from the public journals.

But the most singular thing is the temperance revolution, and the wonder of the age is Father Mathew. I have heard and seen him very satisfactorily, and think with his audiences that it was the greatest spectacle I ever witnessed. To-day I sat very near him by means of Father O'Reilly, and not only saw the whole, but took notes of all his sermon, which was excellent. He is a good looking man about forty-five, florid face, curly black hair, and a Roman nose, with a good-humored expression. He was rather late, owing to the pressure of the people, but when he stepped upon the platform, every voice was hushed and all eyes fixed upon him. If he had been an angel from heaven he would not have commanded more attention. I never saw anything like it before. The band of music played a hymn, during which he stood leaning on the altar, looking over the immense concourse, without seeming to feel any awkwardness or any desire to make a display. His dress was a white robe with gold around the neck and on the streamers in front, and his whole appearance was elegant and pleasing. Some poor cripples, who had been laid inside the railing, were kneeling as well as they could, and muttering their prayers to him, of which he took no notice. After the hymn he stood out more in front, and delivered his text and sermon, without book or notes. This was sensible and suited to the audience, who showed their approbation by frequent responses and prayers at the end of the sentences. This lasted half an hour, during which time I do not think there was a dry eye in the whole assembly, and many were sobbing aloud, I could not tell why, except for the excitement. He then retired, and the meeting adjourned to a large open place,

called the Battery, on the outskirts of the
town.   Here on the rising ground he ad-
dressed them more particularly on the subject of temperance, and administered the
pledge; the rush to take this was almost
fearful, so that the one or two hundred citizen constables were obliged to lay about
them with their poles, to prevent being over-
thrown, and some were seriously injured.
Father O'Reilly and some others near him
constantly shed tears at this sight, which
was extraordinary indeed. For a long distance around, the hills were covered with
people, dressed in their best clothes (which
are not very good). The women with their
white caps and bright red cloaks gave a gay
appearance to the whole. But the most
striking feature in the scene was the sick;
these were brought on carts and in litters,
and were laid about everywhere upon the
grass; their friends were lifting some up
on their shoulders, that the sight of the
Father might cure them; some were too
weak to hold up their heads, and made a
ghastly appearance as they were raised up
to the light; some seemed in the last stage,
and required all the attention of their relations. It was a touching scene to see the

eager anxiety of the mothers and sisters, and to hear their prayers for their sons, husbands, and fathers. One was carried back to the times of the Apostles, and could hardly realize that he was not listening to some inspired person. After seeing the administering of the pledge (which is kept much more sacredly than in the United States), I went around to hear the conversation of the people, and to ascertain if possible how they were affected. I found they were talking of the death of a man in Dublin, who had broken the pledge, and run mad (which was correct), the discourse, and the cures. "It is indeed wonderful," said a country proprietor named O'Ferren, with whom I became acquainted, "how these cures take place; the only encouragement Father Mathew has ever given these poor invalids is that he will pray for them, and yet they believe he can cure by his word or touch, and I know of two boys who were made well in an hour after taking hold of his robe." Seeing three decent-looking men talking together, I asked one if any person had been cured to-day. "I know only one," said the man, "but I presume there are more." "Have you seen the person?" said

I. "Seen him! and have n't I seen him these three years every day, and never knew him walk a step, and is n't he there now jumping about with them boys yonder?" There was no resisting such evidence as this, and as the boy disappeared in the crowd I had no opportunity of disbelieving. I asked a poor woman, who had brought her son ten miles on her back, if she noticed any change in him. "Not yet," she said; "if it 's God's will, he will be cured; we cannot have all we ask for. I hope Father Mathew's prayers may prevail, or at least the sight of such an inspired man may do him good." More than a million adults have taken the pledge, and it is very seldom broken; many say there never has been but one case, — that of the man in Dublin who died, — which shows that there have been but few. Those who take it receive a medal, which they wear around their necks, and many consider it a kind of charm. Father Mathew's likeness is hung in every cottage. . . .

Your affectionate son,

A. A. L.

V.

1841–1853.

On his return from Europe Mr. Lawrence immediately took up the activities of business and society. But he soon felt that the attachments and sympathies of a home were needed to fill out his life. His journal records more and more frequent visits to the house of Mr. William Appleton, to whose daughter, Sarah Elizabeth, he soon became engaged. On March 31, 1842, they were married, in Mr. Appleton's house on Beacon Street, by the Rev. A. H. Vinton, who had just taken charge of St. Paul's Church.

Soon after, they moved to Pemberton Square, which was their home until his love for the country drew Mr. Lawrence and his family outside the city limits.

About a year after his marriage, Mr. Lawrence made an important change in his business relations, and from that time he seems to have really felt that he had seized upon his life work. His journal gives the record of the formation of his business firm.

"May 18, 1843. Robert Mason and myself have decided to make a partnership and run for luck to get the Cocheco Company."

"May 26. The Directors of the Cocheco Company voted to give their business to Mason & Lawrence to-day. I have spoken for some signs and written to Robert to come on here."

"May 29. Signed articles of copartnership with Robert Mason. I deem this a highly important step in my career, and I pray that I may be true to the new duties I have undertaken, and may not allow indolence or timidity to hinder me from taking my full share of the labor which will fall upon me. I know that our success depends very much on our own efforts, and I trust that if it should come, I may not forget my duty in using it, not for my own aggrandizement, but for the advancement of Christ's kingdom upon earth. I hope to look to God for strength and for success; on Him I will lean."

Like every good business man, Mr. Lawrence believed strongly in system; the whole concern, even to its smallest details, should run like a machine ; but he also believed in placing trustworthy men who were in sympathy with his methods, in the responsible positions. Having found his men, he gave them liberal salaries and large freedom of action. He was thus able to reduce the length of his business hours; and his judgment of ability and character was such that he soon drew about him men who remained for many years. After three years of active partnership, Mr. Mason was obliged by his wife's health to pass most of his time in Europe, so that upon Mr. Lawrence fell the management of the firm's business. Mr. H. B. Mather, who was taken into partnership a few years later, took full charge of the accounting department, and was, until his death in 1884, a faithful assistant. Mr. J. D. W. Joy was also a partner for fourteen years, retiring in 1866.

The Cocheco Company, of which Mason & Lawrence were the selling agents, was a corporation for the manufacture and printing of cotton cloths, and at that time was losing money heavily ; very soon after the change of management, Mr. Lawrence was able to report that " the company had made six per cent. on the capital stock in the past six months." Soon the success was such that the firm organized the purchase of the Salmon Falls Company, and, increasing the stock to $300,000, rebuilt the mill.

The selling agency of these two mills Mr. Lawrence held for over forty years, during which the works of both corporations trebled. During most of that time he was director in both corporations, and for some years was treasurer of the Salmon Falls and president of the Cocheco.

With the first directions to the agent at Salmon Falls went this letter from Mr. Lawrence, which suggests his interest in the welfare of the mill-hands : —

"The accompanying pamphlet represents the growing evils which attend the increase of a manufacturing town so clearly, that it reminds one of the importance of beginning right in Salmon Falls. I hope you will keep your attention directed to this point; and if any measures are required to prevent their occurrence, beyond what have already been taken, please to suggest them. In regard to religious instruction, it seems to me that if our church does not produce the desired interest, either from want of talent in the preacher or from prejudice against the forms, there must be some kind of preaching, and some form adopted, which will;" and later, he records, " Went to see the Bishop this week about sending a Roman Catholic clergyman down to Salmon Falls to look after the spiritual interests of the girls, of whom one third are Irish."

Mr. Lawrence's resolution in college not to be a plodding, narrow-minded business man was a principle for life. Charitable and public interests had their immediate claim upon his attention, and before he was able to respond largely with money he gave his time.

For six years he was a trustee of the Massachusetts General Hospital, and took great interest in his regular visits to the Hospital and McLean Asylum.

His work for the colonization of free blacks in Liberia brought frequent applications to his office. " A good-looking black preacher," he records in his journal, " came to get some money to free his family of eleven and take them to Liberia. He required $6,000. He had just heard of the death of his youngest daughter and his heart was tender. I found a tear in my own eye, and he took my hand as he went out, saying, 'I think you are my friend,' which quite choked me up.   Such cases grow more frequent."

" Went round last evening with Bishop McIlvaine of Ohio, begging for his institution."

" The Young Men's Benevolent Society chose me president again."

" Forenoon, went to police court with Mr. Stone to prosecute a man for inhumanly beating his horses."

" Very busy all day with the subscription book for an Episcopal City Mission Chapel: succeeded pretty well."

The following characteristic letter suggests the memory of a unique and kindly character, familiar to every Harvard student of the last generation.

TO PROFESSOR SALES.

Boston, *December* 31, 1852.

MY DEAR SIR, — Will you accept the above (check for $50.00) as a New Year's present from one of your old scholars, who though he did not learn much Spanish, could not help learning to love an instructor so disinterested, so kind, so gentle, so playful, and yet so venerable.   May God grant you, my dear sir, all his consolations here and hereafter.   With great regard,

Yours very truly,   A. A. L.

A mixed education in Unitarianism and Orthodoxy is not usually conducive to a settled faith, and is more likely to lead to argument than to piety. Mr. Lawrence had passed through the argumentative phase, and as a result had written, " Would that I had a Creed; " but that deep and sincere faith which was found in the Unitarianism as well as the Orthodoxy of that day was Mr. Lawrence's by inheritance, education, and conviction. His devotional spirit had sent him to the Prayer Book, which led him into closer sympathy with the Episcopal Church. The result is seen in the record of his journal.

" May 29, 1842. To-day we were both confirmed at St. Paul's Church by Bishop Griswold. There were forty-three others ; among them my brother William and his wife and Marianne Appleton. Our pastor, Dr. Vinton, has labored very successfully. God has poured out his Spirit over the whole country, and there seems to be a universal revival. I pray that we may not either of us ever be led astray by the allurements of this world and forget our God and Saviour."

His practical spirit immediately led him to take hold of the church work.

"Sunday. Went to Sunday-school, St. Paul's: shall have a class next week, of poor children if I can get them. It seems to me the good done by Sunday instruction away from home may be very much increased by taking the poor. 1. It teaches the others that the poor are as good as themselves and may attain even higher moral excellence. 2. If brought together in such a way as not to wound the pride of the richer, there will probably spring up a sympathy for the poorer. 3. It will prevent the jealousy which springs up in the minds of the poor, or at least diminish it. 4. It will make them endeavor to resemble the rich in their good manners and refinement. 5. The acquaintance made at school will often be the cause of their advancement in their trades from the interest which naturally continues for schoolmates, especially those who have imbibed together religious sentiments."

A few days after moving into Pemberton Square he writes, "Yesterday I had a number of poor boys in the lower parlor, whom I hope to teach something. They live about Hatter's Square, are Catholics and cannot all read, and are pretty dirty. They promised to come again Sunday morning, and I have purchased a little bundle of books for them."

The week-day evening lecture at St. Paul's, as well as the two Sunday services, were to him as important as any business engagement. The following extracts from his journal and from a letter to his old schoolmate, William Le Baron, suggest the record of these active and happy years.

"February 17, 1850. . . . My attention is so much taken up with business during the week that I find it very difficult to give it to the more important duties of Sunday. My mind runs away from its devotions to the plans of business and various engagements. I pray God to forgive my frivolity and weakness, and help me to think more of spiritual things. By way of ascertaining whether I have not assumed more responsibility than is consistent with a proper regulation of the time and the thoughts, I have enumerated them as follows: 1. My business of commission merchant with a large establishment, clerks, etc., and but one partner. 2. Office of treasurer of a large manufacturing corporation with a capital of a million of dollars. 3. Director in ten corporations: some of them very large, viz.:

Suffolk Bank (eleven years); Massachusetts General Hospital; Cocheco Company; American Insurance Office; Boston Water Power Corporation; Amesbury Company; Middlesex Canal; Massachusetts Bible Society; Massachusetts Board of Domestic Missions; Groton Academy. 4. I have charge of all my father's property; also Mrs. Luther Lawrence's and Mrs. Seaver's. 5. Of my own property; including lands in the West, the building of a Seminary and a town (Appleton) in Wisconsin, which is a complicated business. Then there is the business of receiving and paying visits, which I do only as much of as is necessary. The membership of various societies requiring some attention; besides my daily duty of giving two hours of daylight to the business of getting exercise enough to keep my body sound. Some trusts I have given up, but others come in to take their place. Is not this too much for one who would improve his mind and his heart, and keep himself ready for a change of scene, and an entrance into the spiritual world? Can one be prepared for higher duties when the mind is filled continually with such thoughts as all these things entail?"

Boston, October 4, 1850.

My dear Le Baron, — . . . Nine years ago I was married to one of the fairest, and one of the least frail, of Eve's frail daughters, Miss Appleton, who has borne me four children, two boys and two girls ; thank God all are living, and they form, with their mother, as happy a family as the world contains. Fortune has never frowned badly, for I have seldom tempted her : so far it has been pretty much sunshine, at least for the last few years. Not having aspired to fame or great wealth, I am not disappointed. My family is too dear to me to allow me to pursue the first, and I am well enough off to be above the temptation of avarice. In the summer I have lived in the country, and, if my life is spared, I hope by another year to make my home there, coming to town every day. In politics I am a moderate Whig, in religion an Episcopalian, and a very indifferent follower of our blessed Master, through whose merits alone we must be saved, if at all.   Your friend,

A. A. L.

From his college days Mr. Lawrence had wished not to live " pent up in the city,"

but " in the country a few miles from town."
In his afternoon rides he was on the watch
for a suitable home, and after two daughters
and two sons were born, he felt that it was
time to carry out his desire.   About two
miles from Boston, by way of the Mill-dam,
was a tract of about ninety acres owned by
Mr. Ebenezer Francis, which, on account of
the one house then standing there, was called
" Cottage Farm."   It adjoined a large tract
owned by Mr. David Sears, who had named
it " Longwood " after the place on St. Hel-
ena where Napoleon died.   This Cottage
Farm near Longwood Mr. Lawrence with
his brother bought, and on his half he built
a stone house in English cottage style, which
from 1851 until his death was his homestead.

The lawn on the south and west was re-
lieved by a grove of oaks on the north,
while on the east was the garden, stocked
in later years with a large variety of fruit,
which in the autumn mornings was distributed to friends and neighbors by Mrs. Lawrence on her way into Boston.

His first act on taking possession of his
house was characteristic.   " 1851, October 5,
Sunday.   A week ago last Wednesday I first
sat at my own table in my own new home.

"Cottage Farm."

My family not having moved here from Mr. Appleton's, I was alone. My man, James, who had come from his farm to live this winter with us, had set the table: he had placed my chair so that I looked out upon the beautiful scene at two windows. As there was no one to sit down but myself, I did not say grace aloud, though I did feel the importance of the change which I had made, and was thankful for having been permitted to make so auspicious a beginning in my new home, probably my home for life, I hope my children's. If so, how many sorrows and how many joys will these walls witness. As soon as James had left the room, I knelt down at the window which looks out into the wood and devoutly thanked God, and invoked his blessing on the house and on all of us. The next day (Thursday, September 25), we all moved in."

A few months later (April 20), he wrote to his uncle, George Richards, in Paris: " The spring is just coming here after a wonderful winter. Even within a fortnight we have had a heavy storm: thirty-six regular snow-storms in all, and good sleighing most of the time. Now we begin to enjoy the country: for my house, although only two miles from Beacon

Street, is as much in the country as though it were twenty. William and myself have ninety acres, and though as to profit we hope to see it occupied, it is more agreeable as a residence as it is now — at least a great part of the year. I have cows, hens, horses, puppies, etc., besides a large family inside the house, and we think nobody lives so pleasantly. Kossuth is here: he receives a kind reception: he is certainly a patriot, though an adventurer, too, and a smart fellow. I think he has reached his zenith of fame."

In those days there was a clear stretch of water on both sides of the Mill-dam from Charles Street to the three roads. Where Commonwealth Avenue now runs, men and boys could almost always be seen in the winter days spearing eels and catching smelts through the ice, or skating across the Back Bay to Roxbury and Brookline. The wind sweeping down the Charles River valley across this long stretch of Mill-dam gave Mr. Lawrence many a rough and cold ride which probably laid up a store of neuralgia for later life.

Though not a robust boy, he had by care and regular exercise developed into a man of more than average strength ; and he had that sensitiveness of nerve and quickness of action which gives success and therefore pleasure in athletic sports.

When in college he wrote, " I am in training to get strength and agility. I am taking some lessons in sparring ; nothing can be of more use to confirm good health or cure it if delicate. I spar with Gray, and am pretty sure of being his equal in a few days, though he is considerably heavier. Then I shall try Thorndike, who has gone through four courses, and is larger in every way and more active." During the winter of 1850 he records : " Afternoon, went to Savin Hill with the club to bowl : snowing very fast all the afternoon. W. D. Sohier, Bartlett, Loring, W. Sohier, lawyers ; G. M. Dexter, J. P. Putnam, and Dr. S. G. Howe."

Skating he kept up until nearly the last winter of his life. Though in these days of excessive attention to athletics the sentiments of the following letter to the Master of Groton Academy seem commonplace, they were not so in 1853 : —

BOSTON, *May* 31, 1853.

DEAR SIR, —The lack of manual labor or of manly and athletic exercises is a source

of weakness and effeminacy in young men,
sometimes inducing disease or aggravating
it. The old English sports, which gave
courage, activity, and strength to our ancestors in the northern country (and which are
still kept up there), qualities which the
hardships of a New England life in the
wilderness sustained for several generations,
have almost died out, excepting among a
few sporting people, and in some schools
where they are kept up under the form of
gymnastics. Exercise, merely as such, becomes irksome; and therefore gymnasiums
have usually been failures. The excitement
of uncertainty is required of a regular game
— a party victorious and a party beaten —
to draw out the energy of body and mind,
to develop the powers of all the limbs and
muscles and quicken the senses. This gives
hardness, and strength, and elasticity of
body (which has its effect upon the mind
and heart) and which few persons ever attain, except during their boyhood and youth.

A good plan for encouraging some of the
most common exercises, such as cricket,
quoits, single-stick, would be to offer a handsome medal for each, to be awarded once in
a year to him who excels; the award to be

made by a jury of his peers, to be chosen by the students at large, each jury containing only those who are not competitors.

These medals, say three, of silver worth twenty dollars each, I propose to furnish.

Yours truly, A. A. L.

He also had the happy faculty of catching a moment's nap at any time and under any circumstances, having such control of himself that he would wake up at a given moment; in fact, during his entrance examination to Harvard College he fell asleep, but hearing the professor say "sufficient" to the student next him, he awoke bright and ready. After coming home tired from business, three minutes on a sofa was enough to rest mind and body and give enjoyment to the afternoon ride. "Generally, when no particular occupation offers I sleep easily in the daytime, though not so well at night; frequently I lie awake several hours in the night after two o'clock. This gives time for reflection which is very useful to me, and no one requires it more. These wakeful seasons may with God's help be the means of keeping religion from dying out in my heart. Never during the day does religion assume such importance as when the world is still and shut out from view; then we weigh the importance of temporal and eternal things more accurately. I pray God that the time may never come to me when these halting places may not occur, affording me an opportunity of looking backward on the past and forward to what is to come."

In 1847 Mr. Lawrence bought a cottage at Lynn just at the head of Long Beach, where its graceful sweep towards Nahant is most marked. And here he passed many summers, reserving a few days in the autumn when he with his family went to renew old associations at the homestead in Groton.

In 1844 his only sister, Mrs. Charles Mason, died, and in 1845 his half-brother Robert, a young man of lovely character, was taken.

The early death of his mother had bound Mr. Lawrence to his father in close affection. Then their common interests in business and philanthropy had caused an association even more intimate. When at Bedford he wrote: "My father has not written me for nearly two weeks, so that I am afraid he is sick. What would become of me if I should lose him! So good a father, so affectionate and watchful of my morals."

With evident gratification he records in 1841: " Father was much pleased with the leading article in the ' Atlas ' yesterday, and more so when I told him it was mine. It was headed ' The Scarcity of Money.' "

The death of his father was, therefore, the great break in his life.

"January 1, 1853. The death of my dear father. I can hardly realize as I write, that the time has come for making this record. It reminds me of many things, but at this moment more particularly of a similar record which my sons must ere long make, — if the life of either of them should be spared a few years, — of my own decease. After many months of improved health, of constant cheerfulness, and of religious and benevolent employment; after receiving a long visit under his own roof from his friends Mr. and Mrs. Pierce, President Hopkins, and others, and in the few days before his last having amended his will, closed the affairs of his partnership of thirty-nine years' standing, paid his almost daily visits to our family here at Longwood, and to my brother's, caressed his grandchildren and kindly greeted many friends, he retired to rest on the night of December 30th in apparently good health.

Soon after midnight he groaned and awakened my mother; but in vain she applied the common restoratives. The life was gone; the soul had gone to God who gave it. Dr. Warren and my brother William were called. Early in the morning William sent out word to me. How many times before I had expected such a sad message, but not now! O God, our Father, grant that we may die as well prepared; that our lives may be as useful; and, if it please Thee, may our death be as free from pain as his."

For several years an enterprise in Wisconsin absorbed much of Mr. Lawrence's time and interest. In the year 1852 the romantic story of "the lost Dauphin" was exciting much interest in this country, and the question was everywhere under discussion, whether the son of Marie Antoinette, the Dauphin of France, who was said to have been spirited away at the time of his mother's death, was not now the Rev. Eleazer Williams, missionary of the Protestant Episcopal Church among the Oneida Indians at their reservation near Green Bay in Wisconsin.

At that time the claims of Mr. Williams, the story of his escape and life among the

Indians, and, more than all, his Bourbon features and noble presence, appealed to the imagination of many.

It was Mr. Lawrence's fortune to see the more prosaic side of Mr. Williams's character. For the pretender to the throne of France had one feature in common with some of his royal cousins: he was in a chronic impecunious condition.

The pressure of circumstances had brought him to Boston as early as 1845 to raise money on five thousand acres of land on which he lived in Wisconsin. Rev. Dr. Lothrop, whose father was also a missionary among the Indians, interested Mr. Amos Lawrence in the matter, but on account of his health the burden of lending the money was taken by his son. The result was that, as the fortune of the lost Dauphin waned, Mr. Lawrence was drawn more and more into the investment, until he found himself the unwilling possessor of over five thousand acres of land in the Fox River Valley, Wisconsin.

Financially, the investment resulted as such forced purchases usually do. The agents turned out careless or dishonest, and the settlers took advantage of a distant owner, until, as Mr. Lawrence wrote, "claims have been laid upon every piece of land which I own in Wisconsin, which has risen in value, while those which have not risen in value remain unmolested."

But the incident has an interest as showing that with the ownership of property came also a sense of responsibility for the welfare of those who lived upon and near it. For as soon as the five thousand acres fell into his hands he wrote to his agent: "I have been thinking more of the establishment of an institution of learning or college on the Williams land, and there seems to be a good opportunity, not only for improving the tone of morals and the standard of education in that vicinity, but also of conferring a lasting benefit on a portion of our countrymen who most need it. I have a high opinion of the adaptation of the principles of the Methodists to the people of the West, and I think, from all that I can learn, that their institutions are carried on with more vigor, and diffuse more good with the same means, than any other. It seems to me decided by experience, that all literary institutions must be controlled by some sect, and efforts to prevent this have often blasted their usefulness.

I should desire most of all to see a Protestant Episcopal institution ; but that is out of the question, as our form of worship is only adopted slowly, and never will be popular in this country. I think the old-fashioned name 'college' or 'school' is as good as any; 'university' would hardly do for such a young child."

Later he wrote: "The school is to be under the control of the Methodist denomination, though it is specified that "a large minority of the trustees shall be from other denominations. I trust it will be conducted so as to do the most good, to diffuse the greatest amount of learning and religion, without reference to propagating the tenets of any sect."

Soon after, Mr. Lawrence yielded to the urgent request of those citizens who were interested in the establishment of a college, to change the location from the Williams tract to the "Grand Chute" on the Fox River, which was considered by them to be a better position. Here a new town was immediately incorporated and named "Appleton," after Mr. Samuel Appleton of Boston, and in it the college was established. Mr. Lawrence's suggestion of the modest title "school" or

" college " was not in accordance with the popular taste for great names, and as he had initiated the movement and had given more than twenty thousand dollars towards its foundation, the charter was obtained under the title " Lawrence University."

For a few years the institution, after the early example and charter of Harvard, educated some of the " Indian youth," but its real work has been in the line of Mr. Lawrence's first suggestion, the diffusion of learning and religion among the people of that vicinity and the neighboring States. Under the successful presidency of his friend, Rev. Dr. Edward Cooke, the university reached a position of influence which it has sustained; and one of the last days of his life was passed in consultation with Dr. Cooke and its present president as to means for increasing its work.

VI.

1854–1856.

In the agitation caused by the passage of the Fugitive Slave Law of 1850, Mr. Lawrence wrote: " Matters of state policy are comparatively of no importance now. The great question is the national one : Shall we stand by the laws or shall we nullify them? Shall we uphold the Union, or shall we break it up ? " Conservative by inheritance and education, he had as little sympathy with the small fraction of " higher law " abolitionists as with their fellow nullifiers, the political leaders of the slaveholders. He could not follow Mr. Webster in his compromises with slavery, but at the same time he esteemed the Free - Soilers a danger to the Union on account of their persistent agitation of the slave question and their sectional spirit. He was a Whig, bound in honor to preserve the original compact of

the Union by which slavery was recognized,
but bound also to use every legitimate means
to prevent the increase of slavery, and ani-
mated with the hope that time and patience
would bring about peacefully the abolition
of the evil. His business acquaintance with
Southern cotton-growers lead him to appreciate their side of the question, and to recognize the care that many of them took in
the welfare of their slaves. " Mr. Carroll
of Carrollton," he wrote, "is staying in
Boston. He was offered $300,000 for the
use of his slaves for five years to be carried
to New Orleans and declined. They earn
nothing more than their support at home.
Would an abolitionist have done it ? " Nevertheless, his active interest in the colony of
freed slaves in Liberia, and in Father Hen-
son and other blacks who were purchasing
freedom for themselves and their families,
kept him alert to the evils of the system.

The great body of conservative, loyal
citizens in the North received a sharp shock
when, in 1854, Congress passed the Kansas-
Nebraska Bill, thus repealing the Missouri
Compromise of 1820.

For twenty-five years North and South
had worked on the common understanding

that there should be no slave State north of
of the line 36° 30′, and the compromise had
gained, in popular esteem, the dignity of a
compact.   When, then, in 1854 Congress cut
Nebraska into halves (calling the southern
half Kansas) and proclaimed the doctrine
of "squatter sovereignty," that each Territory had full control over its own domestic
institutions and could vote for or against slavery without regard to the line of 1820, the
people of the North began to realize that
they had an uncompromising party to deal
with.

It happened that a few weeks after the
passage of the bill a slaveholder, Colonel
Suttle of Alexandria, made a demand on
the authorities in Boston for the delivery of
a runaway slave named Burns who was concealed in the city.   The request did not
tend to calm the irritated spirits of the Boston people.   Three years before, when there
was danger of a mob on account of the delivery of a slave, Mr. Lawrence had offered
his services to United States Marshal Dev-
ens ; but circumstances had changed and
feelings were aroused in 1854.   Mr. Lawrence wrote to the mayor that he " would
prefer to see the court house razed rather

than that the fugitive now confined there should be returned to slavery." In a letter to his brother he said: "The newspapers will give you an account of the slave excitement here. I tell you it was high times. Mayor Smith called out all the troops in this region, and it was a regular muster day when the fugitive was carried off; all business was suspended. The negro was a good-looking fellow and well dressed; and as he marched down State Street in the procession, cavalry and artillery with cannon and United States troops were before and behind him; but he held his head up and marched like a man. The windows and houses were filled with people, though the streets and even the cross streets had all been cleared. The blood of '76, like that of St. Januarius, boiled up, and it was nothing but the clearing of the streets previously and the immense display of military that prevented the total destruction of the United States marshal and his hired assistants."

The passage of the Kansas - Nebraska Bill turned the eyes of the whole country upon the new Territory, Kansas, which was placed in a unique and critical position. The scattered settlers in a great Territory, which, until the passage of this bill, had been an Indian reservation, were to have the privilege of deciding by popular vote whether slavery or freedom should exist in its borders. The slave and free powers in the nation were so evenly balanced that the decision of Kansas became of national importance. It was the first open popular struggle, which ended in the civil war. Immediately that rough body of men which hover around the borders of every new country pushed in and drove down stakes. Drawn largely from the Southern country, their influence was pro-slavery. Soon the adjoining slave State, Missouri, realized the necessity of having her neighbor in agreement with herself, and across her borders swarmed a very uncomfortable looking lot of settlers, who had at least one firm conviction, that Kansas must go pro-slavery. Certainly every appearance was in their favor. In a few weeks the people of the North began to realize that Kansas needed Free State settlers. Still, slavery had every advantage, and the country was about to settle down to the fact of another slave Territory, when Mr. Eli Thayer of Worcester suggested the idea of organized emigration for

Kansas. Even before the passage of the Kansas-Nebraska Bill he had obtained a charter for the " Massachusetts Emigrant Aid Association," allowing a capital of five million dollars, with the intention of controlling all emigration in the interest of liberty. His hope was first to secure all the Territories and then move upon the slave States, — a plan more magnificent in idea than in immediate possibilities. The critical situation of Kansas, however, gave a practical turn to the scheme. Here was an opportunity for lovers of freedom to fight for their cause in a legitimate and thoroughly American way, by creating public opinion in a Territory through the encouragement of the settlement of *bonâ fide* citizens and legal voters. Having accepted the position as one of the three trustees of the association at the request of his friend, Mr. Patrick Jackson, Mr. Lawrence found to his surprise that he had undertaken a piece of work which was as arduous as it was expensive.

A short experience proved that the original scheme was too magnificent in its scope, and a new and more practical constitution was drawn up. The design of the revised

association, called " The New England Emigrant Aid Company," was " to promote the
emigration to Kansas Territory of persons
opposed to slavery there, and to prevent, by
all legal and constitutional means, its establishment there as well as in the Territory
of Nebraska." Its immediate objects were
" to procure for such emigrants cheap fare
and good accommodations on the route, to
advise them, through agents, on their arrival
out, in regard to eligible sites for settlements; to secure for their benefit, by purchase or otherwise, advantageous locations
as landing-places, a general rendezvous for
outfitting purposes, etc.; to erect receiving
houses for the temporary convenience for
settlers' families; to establish furnishing
stores, at which, on reasonably low terms,
the necessaries and comforts of life may be
pnrchased; to erect, or aid individuals in
erecting and conducting, saw-mills, grist-
mills, machine-shops, and similar establish-
ments, essential in new settlements; to in-
troduce the printing press, and thus afford
a medium of communication between the
settlers, their friends, and the public."

To accomplish these and kindred objects,
the trustees proposed to raise the sum of

$200,000, for which they looked to the liberality of all disposed to aid in the cause. To contributors they issued certificates of loans representing twenty dollars each.

Mr. Lawrence never shared the expectation of some of his associates, that the stock would pay dividends, or even that the stockholders would ever see their money again, and he would have preferred to depend upon the gifts of patriotic citizens without entering into such financial obligations. To his father's old friend, Professor Packard of Bowdoin College, he wrote : "The shape in which it is presented is objectionable, that is, as a stock company, and it imposes on those who manage it the responsibility of making dividends or of becoming odious. It was with great reluctance that I meddled with it at all ; but it was just about dying for want of concerted action and for want of money and business knowledge on the part of those who had started it. Even now it is sickly for want of funds, but it has given an impulse to emigration into Kansas which cannot easily be stopped."

To a clergyman who asked his advice about investing in the stock, he answered : " Keep your money for your own use, rather than do anything of that sort. The value of land stock companies is the most delusive of all stocks; and persons are more easily drawn into them than any other. Some of my coadjutors in this enterprise would, if they had the money, invest large sums in this stock; but fortunately the sanguine ones who have property are all in debt, and the poorer ones must rest content. I have taken considerable, but only so much as I am willing to contribute to the cause; and I have already given a part of this away, and intend to do the same with the balance."

However, with Mr. John Carter Brown of Providence as president, he accepted the position of treasurer and trustee, in association with the two other trustees, Messrs. Eli Thayer and J. M. S. Williams.

On the 17th of July, 1854, the first party of twenty-nine emigrants were cheered out of the railroad station by their friends and the trustees, and on the 29th of August a second party of seventy, which was increased very much on the route, moved out of Boston singing, to the tune of " Auld Lang Syne," one of the " Lays of the Emigrants " written for the occasion by Mr. Whittier : —

> " We cross the prairie as of old
>   The Pilgrims crossed the sea,
>   To make the West, as they the East,
>   The homestead of the free!
>
> " We go to rear a wall of men
>   On Freedom's southern line,
>   And plant beside the cotton-tree
>   The rugged Northern pine! "

To the record of their departure Mr. Lawrence added: " All the expenditure thus far has been met by myself, but I cannot go farther without funds in hand. These must be raised soon. The stock remains as it was: only $20,000 taken." A few days after, he was able to give this report of doubtful encouragement: "$50,000 of our stock has been taken, thereby enabling us to make an assessment. But it was done by a forced process, — the trustees taking $10,000 more each, which they are responsible for."

As the pro-slavery squatters had settled in little towns on the borders near Missouri, the first object of the New England emigrants was to create a centre for the anti-slavery settlers. The conductor of the first party, C. H. Branscomb, therefore followed the directions given him from Boston, and went up the Kansas River. Soon a camp of tents, increased later by huts and log-cabins, marked the settlement of Wakarusa. A village with an Indian title seemed to the settlers hardly consistent with the dignity of the rising "city," and they naturally turned to the East for a name. In answer to a request for a fitting title Mr. Lawrence had written : "It is my decided opinion that the Indian names of places, if they are not too harsh, are the best." But Dr. Charles Robinson, who was the leading representative of the Emigrant Aid Company, answered : "Your letter came too late to influence the action of the citizens. A letter from Mr. Thayer was received some time since, offering a library on behalf of the citizens of Worcester, if the city would be called by that name ; but our people are nearly unanimous in their opposition to the names of Eastern or other cities for our city. Most of our people are very much attached to your name, and after I had explained your course in connection with our enterprise, and your personal characteristics, as they had been exhibited to me, there was much enthusiasm manifested, and I think it will be impossible to induce our people to change the name of their city for any considerations."

Mr. Lawrence again protested: "My motives, thus far, have been pure and unselfish; and I wish them not only to be, but to *appear*, so; this would not be the case, should it be made public that the settlement had been named for me. It would give to my future efforts the appearance of promoting my own celebrity, — or, in other words, my own interests, — and would lessen my own influence for the good of the cause. Besides this, it might excite dissatisfaction in the minds of my associated trustees, both of whom are devoted to it, and one of whom labored in it long before I did."

But he was met by the final letter from a committee of citizens: "We thought that one who, in the darkest hour of the grand enterprise, stepped nobly forth to urge on its lagging energies and nerve it with the firm 'sinews of war,' and who entered without the hope or expectation of remuneration, was worthy of lasting remembrance. It is for these, with other reasons, dear sir, that we have taken the liberty of calling our already important place Lawrence."

The purchase of a hotel in Kansas City, Mo., for the temporary lodgment of emigrants, the incidental expenses, and agents' salaries, brought steady demands on the trustees. Mr. Thayer went from city to city, stating the purpose of the society, creating branch societies, and recruiting emigrants; while in Boston Messrs. Lawrence and Williams tried to raise the necessary funds, though the association was most of the time six or seven thousand dollars in debt to the treasurer. It was also easier for those who talked to make promises than for the treasury to meet them. " There is a good deal of bluster," wrote Mr. Lawrence to Mr. John Carter Brown, " in regard to the movements of this company, and statements as to the magnitude of our plans which are untrue." To Mr. Pomeroy, an agent in Kansas, he sent word, " This makes over-drafts for about $6,000. As to obtaining money, I am sorry to say the prospect under our present arrangement is very poor; some change must be made. Meantime we are making large promises as to what we will do for settlers which are certain to be broken, and which will entail much dissatisfaction." " The labor is much greater than you would suppose," he informed Mr. Williams, " fully as much as to be treasurer of a manufacturing corporation with a capital of $1,500,000." At about the same time his journal reads: " Kansas drafts came in ; no money in the treasury and never have had, and no money of my own. So I transferred some manufacturing company's stock to be sold and pay them. If Kansas should not be a free State, I shall lay it to heart and to my pocket too."

The report of the Massachusetts emigration movement was spread through the country with great exaggerations, so that the Southern politicians found in it a ready excuse for pouring ruffians across the line simply to vote; and though the abolitionists condemned this constitutional method of creating free States as " false in principle," yet it was heralded as an abolitionists' movement. Several congressmen had attacked the association so savagely that Mr. Lawrence felt bound to justify to Mr. Benton the company's action.

Boston, *January* 2, 1855.

Dear Sir, — . . . It has been asserted that the emigrants have had their expenses paid to go to Kansas and vote. In your published speech you say that the same game may have been played on both sides.

As you love to know the truth and to defend it, I will state that not one man has gone from New England who has had his expenses paid, even in part. I am the treasurer and a trustee of the only New England society which has sent out settlers, and know that all the money collected has been spent in erecting school-houses, temporary huts, steam saw and grist mill, in purchasing a tavern in the town of Kansas, Mo., and for similar purposes, and for nothing worse.

In soliciting subscriptions or receiving them, it is usual to allow the subscriber to take and pay for it as stock, say $200, and to receive a certificate of it, as in any other stock company; or to give outright, for the same, $100. Many prefer to give the money; that is, they do not value the stock at half price. None has ever been sold, nor would it sell at over one half; nor do I believe that there is a stockholder who would not have taken three fourths of the cost the moment when he paid the money. It is what those who favor it call a " patriotic " movement, to bring into active and healthy life a new State, and to keep slavery out of it; to get good institutions *in*, and to keep a bad institution *out*. Those "sent out" have not been abolitionists; so far as we know, not one known to be of that stamp has gone in our parties. They are free to vote and to do as they please. The society has no agreement with them nor pledge, nor are they asked any questions; since it is presumed that all New England men think alike about the iniquity of the measure of the last session, and as you do.

Yours truly,   A. A. L.

President Pierce was only too ready to listen to the Southern statement of the Kansas difficulties; but as he happened to be a nephew of Mr. Lawrence's mother, the connection gave Mr. Lawrence opportunities to try and correct the false impressions. "I have been pained often," he wrote to the President, "by seeing this association misrepresented; it has been called an affair of the abolitionists, etc. Some societies under this name have been formed by abolitionists, but have accomplished nothing."

In the mean time, affairs were approaching a crisis in Kansas. Three months after the first party arrived, they had their first experience of a Kansas election. The choice of a delegate to Congress for a fractional term was not a great issue, but it was enough to bring seventeen hundred and twenty-nine Missourians across the border to have a picnic and stuff the ballot - boxes. The pro-slavery candidate was therefore elected. As the question of slave State or free State depended on the legislature, the capture of that body in the second election was worth a struggle. Even the Senator from Missouri, then acting vice-president, David R. Atchison, did not consider the subject beneath his notice and personal activity. The result was that on the morning of the 30th of March the taverns of Kansas were put to the test to supply food and liquor for the five thousand new citizens who, armed with revolvers and bowie-knives, had swarmed in from Missouri to exercise the privilege of American citizens, and to vanish across the border in the evening. A total of sixty - three hundred and seven votes in a Territory including only twenty-nine hundred and five legal voters was rather trying. In anticipation of this Mr. Lawrence had written to Mr. Atchison : —

(COTTAGE FARM NEAR) BOSTON, *March* 31, 1855.

MY DEAR SIR, — I take the liberty to address you upon a subject in which I have a common interest with yourself, viz.: the settlement of Kansas. Since the repeal of the " Missouri Compromise " by the last Congress, this Territory has attracted the attention of distant not less than of the neighboring States; for it is evident that there must be decided the question whether there shall be slave or free labor over a vast region of the United States now unsettled. You and your friends would make slave States, and we wish to prevent your doing so. The stake is a large one, and the ground chosen. Let the fight be a fair one.

It is to secure this that I address you. Your influence is requisite to restrain your people from doing great injustice to actual settlers, and provoking them to retaliatory measures, the consequences of which would be most deplorable. I beg you, my dear sir, to use your efforts to avert so great an evil.

Let the contest be waged honorably, for unless it be so, no settlement of the question can ever be final. It is already reported here that large bodies of Missourians will cross over merely to vote, and that they may gain this election as they did the last. But how delusive to suppose that settlers who have come from one to two thousand miles with their families will acquiesce in any election gained by such means, or that any future election can be satisfactory which is not conducted according to law. The advantage of proximity is yours; your people can afford to be not only just, but generous, in this matter. The repeal of the law which secured this Territory against the introduction of slavery is considered by most men in the " free States " to be a breach of the national faith ; and it is not unreasonable for those who have gone there to find a home to expect a compliance with the laws as they are. Those from New England have gone in good faith and at their own expense. They are chiefly farmers ; but among them are good representatives from all professions. Some have considerable property, but all have rights and principles which they value more than money, and, I may say, *more than life itself.* Neither is there any truth in the assertion that they are abolitionists. No person of that stripe is known to have gone from here ; nor is it known here that any such have gone from other States. But oppression may make them abolitionists of the most dangerous kind.

There has been much said in regard to an extensive organization here, which is wholly untrue. I assure you, sir, that what has been undertaken here will be carried on fairly and equitably. The management is in the hands of men of prudence, of wealth and determination; they are not politicians, nor are they aspirants for office: they are determined, if it be possible, to see that justice is done to those who have ventured their all in that Territory. May I not hope, sir, that you will second this effort to see that the contest shall be carried on fairly? If fairly beaten you may be sure that our people will acquiesce, however reluctant; but they never will yield to injustice.

Respectfully yours,   A. A. L.

Soon after he wrote to President Pierce:

BOSTON, *April* 17, 1855.

MY DEAR SIR, — As the subject of the recent election in Kansas Territory will probably be brought to your notice officially, and as various accounts of it will be written by interested parties, it may not be amiss for me to state very briefly what I know to be true.

Having been in a situation to see many

private letters from persons in various parts of the Territory, most of them indicating intelligence and fairness, and having conversed with an intelligent man just from there, I consider it proved conclusively that the proceedings of the Missourians who crossed over with arms were a series of outrages, grossly insulting to the actual settlers, to the government, and to the public sentiment of the whole country. It is difficult to imagine that so much injury could have been inflicted unaccompanied by serious casualties, and it can only be accounted for from the fact that the invading force was overwhelmingly large.

Since Governor Reeder has declined to be used as the agent of this illegal combination, he has been pursued by the foulest slander, and now by threats. He will require all the countenance and support of the government to sustain him in the position in which he is placed in the performance of his duty.

Respectfully and truly yours,

A. A. L.

In a few months the citizens of Kansas found themselves with a legislature which, though repudiated by the territorial governor, Reeder, imported the whole code of Missouri into Kansas. This body of law-makers not only legalized slavery, but denounced death against any one who aided in the escape of a slave. As Professor Spring in his " History of Kansas " writes : " Their code struck at the liberty of the press, at freedom of speech, and the sanctities of the ballot-box."

The Emigrant Aid Company sent only about thirteen hundred emigrants. But the patriotic motive behind it affected public opinion over the country and helped to make the Kansas struggle of national interest. The emigrants, too, were of such character and spirit that they formed the nucleus of the Free State movement, and their city, Lawrence, was its headquarters. One of the happiest results, however, was the choice of Dr. Charles Robinson of Fitchburg as the principal agent of the company in Kansas. Having had some experiences in California in the early mining days, he now developed a power of leadership which made him the centre and guide of the Free State citizens. He soon wrote to Mr. Lawrence, " Instead of recognizing this as the legislature of Kansas and participating in its proceedings as such, I utterly repudiate it." "Simply as a citizen and as a man, I shall, therefore, yield no submission to this alien legislature."

A few days after the receipt of this letter an entry in Mr. Lawrence's journal runs: "Paid $1,000 for rifles for Kansas sufferers; proceeds of them, when sold, to go to the 'Church of the Pilgrims' in Kansas." And he then wrote to President Pierce: —

Boston, July 15, 1855.

My dear Sir, — It is evident that there is a body of men in Missouri who are determined to drive our people from Kansas, if they dare to do so; and for the reason that the settlers from the "free States" are opposed to the introduction of slave trade there. Up to this time the government has kept so far aloof as to force the settlers to the conclusion that if they would be safe, they must defend *themselves;* and therefore many persons here who refused at first (myself included) have rendered them assistance, by furnishing them the means of defense.

Yours with regard,   A. A. L.

Then he wrote to Dr. Webb, secretary of the Emigrant Aid Company: —

Boston, *July* 20, 1855.

Dear Doctor, — Here is a letter which indicates that the crisis approaches, and it shows that our friend Robinson is the man to meet it. That a revolution must take place in Kansas is certain, if that can be called a revolution which is only an over-throw of usurpation. When farmers turn soldiers they must have *arms*. Write to Hartford and get their terms for one hundred more of the Sharps rifles at once.

Yours truly,   A. A. L.

On the same day he wrote to Dr. Robinson: —

Boston, *July* 20, 1855.

My dear Sir, — You are on the eve of stirring times. I wish Mr. Pomeroy was with you. I wish we *all* were there, if we could stand up like men to the work in hand. I know more than one man here, who looks every day and every night at his wife and little ones, and doubts which way his duty lies. But we must not doubt. Young men and men like you must do the work, and you must have the glory of saving a good part of your country to freedom. But you must have arms, or your courage will not avail. We must stir ourselves here to-morrow and see what can be done.

Yours faithfully, ·A. A. L.

On the promise from Mr. Lawrence of $1,000 for arms, Dr. Samuel Cabot, who was one of the directors of the Emigrant Company, immediately started a subscription paper and obtained $1,600 more from a small but mixed company of hunkers, republicans, and abolitionists, — Samuel A. Eliot, J. M. Forbes, Wendell Phillips, Gerritt Smith, John Bertram, Cunningham Brothers, Theodore Lyman, Henry Lee, E. Rockwood Hoar, Samuel Hoar, G. Howland Shaw, William R. Lawrence, and two or three others.

At the same time Mr. J. B. Abbott appeared in Boston with letters from the Kansas people asking for arms. Mr. Lawrence immediately gave him this order to Mr. Palmer of the Sharps rifle manufactory at Hartford: —

"Request Mr. Palmer to have one hundred Sharps rifles packed in casks like hard-

ware and to retain them subject to my order. Also to send the bill to me by mail. I
will pay it either with my note, according
to the terms agreed on between him and Dr.
Webb, or in cash, less interest at seven per
cent."

Before the subscriptions had come in,
Mr. Lawrence had advanced the payment
by his note for $2,700; for, as he wrote to
his uncle, " I send to Kansas every hundred
dollars that I can get and which is not
previously engaged ; for that seems to be an
immediate necessity and will not bear de-
lay." A few casks marked " books " were
soon on their way to Kansas, and later,
several " boxes of primers " were received
by the Free State citizens for the education
of their Missouri neighbors. They arrived
just in time for service. President Pierce,
instead of listening to the urgent requests
of the citizens of Kansas for justice and protection, had dismissed Governor Reeder, and
had put in his place Wilson Shannon. The
new governor immediately yielded to his pro-
slavery advisers, and, taking advantage of
exaggerations, ordered out the state militia
(which consisted largely of Missouri ruffians) for the invasion of the Free State

headquarters, — the city of Lawrence. To their surprise they found five small forts garrisoned with six hundred men, two hundred of whom were armed with Sharps rifles. The major-general, Dr. Robinson, had never seen military service, but he had that tact and shrewdness which gave him a bloodless victory. In the midst of the excitement he wrote to Mr. Lawrence : —

LAWRENCE, *December 4, 1855.*

DEAR SIR, — We are invaded by order of Governor Shannon, but all will be right, I think. I have only time to thank you and the friends who sent us the Sharps rifles, for they have given us, and will give us, the victory without firing a shot. We need, however, one or two hundred more of the same sort.

In haste, very respectfully,

C. ROBINSON.

Fearing that the excitement of the Kansas people might lead them to resist the United States government, Mr. Lawrence in sending the first instalment of rifles had written Dr. Robinson : —

BOSTON, *August* 10, 1855.

MY DEAR SIR, — From Mr. Abbott who has just arrived here from your neighborhood, I infer that the spirit of the settlers has been raised so high that they are ready to repudiate the present legislature altogether, and to resist its requirements. In this, you will have the good-will and assistance of the citizens of the free States at least.

But many are willing to go farther, and to resist the United States government, if it should interfere. For this I can see no apology; nor can there ever be good cause for resisting an administration chosen by ourselves. However wrong in our opinion, there never can be good reason for resisting our own government, unless it attempts to destroy the power of the people through the elections, that is, to take away the power of creating a new administration every four years. But I do not believe the present administration will attempt to impose the Missouri code upon the citizens of Kansas.

There is another reason of a more prudential kind, viz.: that whoever does this is sure of defeat. We are a law-abiding people, and we will sustain our own govern-

ment "right or wrong." Any movement
aimed at the government destroys at once
the moral force of the party or organization
which favors it. Already the present administration is rendered powerless by the
House of Representatives, and soon will
come the time to vote for a new one. The
people will never resist or attempt to destroy it in any other way.

Yours very truly, A. A. L.

A few days later he wrote: "To set up
for yourselves is to dispute the power of the
United States government, and that is a
thing which never will be approved in this
country, I hope. Perhaps this is not a
correct view of the case. But if it is, there
can be no difference of opinion. The sentiment of the whole free States is right on
this subject; democrats and all think alike.
Nothing should be done to make a division.
Prudence, Doctor, forbearance, and decision,
these are the qualities which will be most
in requisition. I feel sure that the United
States government never will undertake to
enforce the whole of the laws of the present
legislature, and perhaps none of them. I
wrote to you on the 10th. Write me a good

letter about the want of the means of defence, and ask Mrs. Nichols to write me one. Dr. Cabot wants them to show, in order to get money for rifles."

The Free State settlers felt that they had the right and duty of self-defence from the incursions of Missouri ruffians, the stuffing of the ballot-boxes, and the execution of the code of laws passed by a bogus legislature, and in this they were encouraged by the sentiment of all liberty-loving citizens. But the distinction between such self-defence and resistance to the United States government, the officers of the Emigrant Aid Company and their agents in Kansas held to be a vital one. And though the charge was then made, and has since been repeated, that the officers and agents of the Emigrant Aid Company encouraged resistance to the United States authority, there is nothing in their correspondence or actions that substantiates the charge. On the contrary, with every new box of rifles went the urgent advice, " Your best friends would advise you, if their opinion was asked, not under any circumstances to resist any legal representative of the United States, nor allow our people to do it. That would put you wrong before the coun-

try, and more than anything else take from you the nationality which you now hold."
" The President is in a bad predicament, as you see by his proclamation. He wants to have the ruffians flogged, but he is afraid to do it. He knows that Free State people are law-abiding, but he is afraid to say that from fear of being called an abolitionist himself. I do hope our friends will never dispute the authority of the United States. It will help the cause, if that sentiment could be brought out in some way, so as not to appear to have been done by design."

To Dr. Robinson he wrote, on December 10, 1855 : —

" To-day newspapers contain the first reliable information in regard to the recent difficulties. We are usually obliged to feed on lies for several days, and so it has been in this case. I do not believe you will have the United States government against you. But if you should, adhere to your determination not to allow any circumstances to lead to a resistance. If the Kansas men are true to the cause of freedom, they will never infringe in the least degree the constitution and laws of the United States. For the part which you have taken, I thank you, my dear sir, from the bottom of my heart, and you will receive the gratitude of all men who like freedom better than slavery."

On the same day he wrote to President Pierce, who had begun to suspect the settlers of treason : —

"From letters which I have seen from the men who exert the most influence in Kansas, and who represent the Free State party there (a party comprising three fourths of the inhabitants), there has been no intention of resisting the execution of the laws of the United States by the proper officers ; nor can any circumstances arise which will induce them to resist, or even to question the authority of the United States Executive.   They will not recognize the late legislature, nor its enactments, nor its officers."

Again : "I believe you do not overrate the intensity of feeling on this subject in the Territory and in the adjoining States ; nor the magnitude of the danger which now threatens the peace of the country from this cause. Preparations are making, on the one side for attack, and on the other for defence ; and if the latter proves ineffectual, we shall, within a few months, see what never has been seen in this country, and what never can be seen but once — an internal civil and servile war. If future history should trace this back to the repeal of the compromise of 1820, your administration, otherwise so honorable, would receive the condemnation of posterity.

" But though we have many national sins to be atoned for, I trust that the same kind Providence which has averted previous dangers to our Union will avert this, and save us from a great national calamity."

Again, to Hon. Gerritt Smith he wrote : "The outcry made by the Administration papers against sending arms is to hide the Administration's neglect to send orders long ago for protecting the settlers. The assertion that they are to be used in resisting the authority of the United States government is wholly unfounded."

Again, when in November, 1856, the probable election of Buchanan caused the fear that what had been gained might in that case be lost, pressure from some of the more enthusiastic advocates of Kansas suggested resistance to the government. At that time Mr. Lawrence made this record in his journal : —

"November 5. Went with Governor Robinson and Senator Henry Wilson to a private meeting of about twenty Kansas men to decide what shall be done if Buchanan is elected. Rev. Mr. Higginson advocated resistance to the government. Mr. Wilson spoke against that doctrine very decidedly: so did I."

The New England Emigrant Aid Company had nothing to do with the purchase of arms for Kansas. A few of the officers of the society, who were in a position to know the needs of Kansas, as private citizens joined with other citizens in the purchase of the arms. Mr. Lawrence was treasurer of the Aid Company, but in speaking of the arms he wrote to Dr. Webb, the secretary of the Company, " Dr. Cabot is treasurer of the rifle funds. I am treasurer of the relief funds."

VII.

1856.

THE affairs of the Free State men in Kansas, who under their own constitution had elected Robinson governor of Kansas in January, 1856, went from bad to worse. The President, whom Mr. Lawrence described as "a small man who held a great office," seemed passive under the pro-slavery influences about him: the territorial government gained courage; and, under Judge Le Compte, the grand jury sent out warrants for the arrest of the leading Free State men as traitors. Lawrence was invaded, the printing press was destroyed, Governor Robinson's house was burned and he was taken prisoner, the hotel and shops were sacked and gutted.

It was, however, a struggle which could be carried on only in Kansas. The Emigrant Aid work was over, and the friends of liberty could only show their interest by giving aid and encouragement to the impoverished, and bringing pressure to bear upon the Executive at Washington. Into this work Mr. Lawrence now entered. To a Quaker at Lynn he wrote a characteristic letter: —

BOSTON, *September* 24, 1856.

MY DEAR SIR, — In reply to yours I will say that all money sent to the treasurer of the New England Emigrant Aid Company (myself) will be appropriated as you request. This company has never sent arms nor ammunition. Any supplies of this sort were sent by private individuals. . . . This company is now forwarding clothing, which is very much wanted to enable the settlers, who have been harassed all summer, and have lost their crops partially or wholly, to remain during the winter. Few have money to spare to lay in a stock of new clothes, and they must buy them at a high price, if at all. We have a depository for all this in Iowa, and it will be used only as it is wanted. *Shoes.* What can Lynn people do so useful as collect all the unsalable shoes, if there are such things, and send them out. They must have them packed in barrels, or you may pack them and mark them LYNN. A dozen or two such boxes would revive their weary *soles.* Send to T. H. Webb, Emigrant Aid Rooms, 3 Winter Street, Boston. Now is the time. All merchandise must go out at once. In many towns the ladies are having "Bees" to sew for Kansas. In some houses (my own for one) they have packed up everything not in use, and will buy a new stock for themselves. Remember that there are thirty thousand Free State men, women, and children there. Take off your coat, my dear friend, and put on your best one: and take your overcoat and pantaloons ; save only one suit for Sunday and week days, and pack up the rest. That will stir up your neighbors to do the same. They will be warmer without them because their hearts will keep them warm all winter, and inside heat is the best and lasts the longest.

Yours very truly,   A. A. L.

To a citizen of Osawatomie, Kansas, he wrote: "At this time there is a great effort making to get enough to rebuild the hotel and to place two more mills where they have been promised. I wish my own means were commensurate with my desires, and I would

do the needful. Some people dread the responsibility imposed by wealth; I have never
had that feeling, but the reverse, for I feel
every day and hour, the want of money.
Twenty times the amount I have to spare
would not come amiss, in fact the want of it
makes me more or less unhappy every day.
This very morning I have declined to do as
much as would require my receipts for many
months."

To the release of Dr. Robinson, Mr. Lawrence gave close attention. He wrote to
Hon. S. G. Haven, member of Congress, " A
friend of mine, Dr. Charles Robinson, one
of the noblest men I ever knew, is at this
moment a prisoner, guarded by the troops of
the Federal Government, though he has
done nothing but what you or I would have
been proud to do. He is not only a patriot,
but he is a lover of the constitution and the
laws. In order to save him from trouble,
I have taken for him, from the commencement, the highest legal advice in Massachusetts, and he has followed it."

Through Mr. Pomeroy of Kansas, who was
now in Washington, Mr. Lawrence tried un-
successfully to move the President to release
Dr. Robinson. But another and more effec-

tive method was used. He first wrote the draught of such a letter as would have been written by a wife imploring the release of her husband. This letter was then copied by Mrs. Robinson, who took the precaution to omit some of the more sentimental passages, and was sent to Mrs. Pierce inclosed with a letter from Mr. Lawrence's stepmother, who was a favorite aunt of the President. Mrs. Pierce after reading the letter handed it to her husband, and a few days later Mr. Lawrence was able to write to Mrs. Robinson, " Not long since the President wrote to my brother that he had given such instructions as would gratify him and his friends here, especially my mother, whose good opinion he valued more than that of all the politicians."

The result was the release of Dr. Robinson.

In a few mouths Kansas seemed to be assured of freedom ; and Mr. Lawrence could write to a Kansas acquaintance in July, 1857 : —

" We look on the great question as now settled, and all political movements in Kansas as having chiefly a local interest. Some of us stood ready to have made a much greater sacrifice had it been necessary, somewhat commensurate with that made by yourself and others. For months I felt as though I held my property and even my life by an uncertain tenure ; but with a numerous family of children and a loving wife, I did not intend to part with either until it was necessary to bring up the 'forlorn hope.' But I have never had the least doubt about our carrying it ultimately. Please not show this to any one, for I never wrote it before, and never reflect upon it without devout gratitude to God for having spared me so great a sacrifice. Now we must be magnanimous to the South. Slavery cannot be extended. Whether it can ever be got rid of in this country is doubtful. It is a curse imposed by the sins of our ancestors, and we must bear it patiently."

In January, 1858, Dr. Robinson sent the welcome news to Mr. Lawrence : "Thank God, the battle is over in Kansas and the victory is won. The Lecompton state government is secured, and now all is in the hands of the people. The border ruffians are now opposing their own constitution."

Eighteen months later, when affairs in Kansas were settled, Governor Robinson in a friendly letter gave this gratifying testimony: " You may not know it and the people of Kansas may not be sensible of it, but I am very much mistaken in my estimate of the influences that have contributed to the freedom of Kansas, if we are not far more indebted to you than to any other man for our success. Without your name, the Emigrant Aid Company would have been a cipher, and without your encouragement, courage, and support, what little I have been able to do would have been left undone."

Time and more mature thought seem only to have deepened the impression of Governor Robinson, who thirty years later writes to Mr. Lawrence's son:

LAWRENCE, KANSAS, *June* 13, 1887.

MY DEAR SIR, — I have said innumerable times that I believe that without the aid rendered by Amos A. Lawrence and Eli Thayer, Kansas would have been a slave State. I think the absence of either would have been fatal. I know of no other man whose presence was indispensable. When the dust of controversy shall have settled or been wiped away, it will be clearly seen that without the movement in New England, embodied in the Emigrant Aid Society, the South would have had an easy victory, and without the material and moral support to that society of Mr. Lawrence and Mr. Thayer, it would have been an abortion. It was his individual money that sent out the first agents, Mr. Branscomb and myself, in June, 1854, within one month after the passage of the Kansas-Nebraska Bill, and my belief is that all the money advanced for months, if not for years, was from his private funds, — that is, the receipts were always behind the expenditures, and the company was always in debt to its treasurer. The moral support his name gave the movement cannot be measured.

Mr. Lawrence was one of the very few men who seemed to comprehend the struggle in its every detail, and to see the end from the beginning. To his mind there were no accidents. Each step taken by the Free State men had a meaning, and every movement of the Free State party was in accordance with a plan well digested and understood by him. Mr. Lawrence was distinguished for many and great virtues and deeds, but the crowning glory of his beneficent life will forever be his work in saving Kansas to freedom, and, as a consequence, redeeming the nation from the curse of slavery.   Very truly,

C. ROBINSON.

The account of Mr. Lawrence's connection with the settlement of Kansas would not be complete without the mention of two points which suggest historic interest as well as some features of his character.

The first is in relation to the education of the people of Kansas. As was seen in Wisconsin, he could not throw money and enthusiasm into the development of a piece of country, or of a struggling population, without, at the earliest moment, laying the foundation of some system of popular education.

The earliest settlers of Kansas, like true New Englanders, had no sooner driven down their tent-pins than they began to talk of a college. Fearing that they might fall into the error of developing a superficial form of higher education before the rudiments had been attended to, Mr. Lawrence wrote to Dr. Robinson in November, 1854 : —

" You have laid out grounds for a college, and will have a good one, without doubt, in time ; but, in the first place, you must have a preparatory school, where the

boys shall be fitted for college. It should
be for boys, and not for girls. There may
be a girls' school too; but the boys should
be cared for first. My own impression is
that we have fallen into a great error here in
Massachusetts, of late years, by raising the
standard of female education so high that
physical development has been checked, and
the constitutions weakened. Our women
are good scholars, and good school-mis-
tresses; but they are unhealthy and weak,
and do not bear strong children; and while
we are refining the intellect, we are injur-
ing the stock. . . .

"I wish my finances were so that I could
give you an order to go on and build at
once; but that is out of the question. My
share in the transaction shall be to pay one
hundred dollars every month, and I think I
can continue to do that, if my health is
spared, for some time to come. The only
condition which shall be imposed is that
you shall not mention to any one, nor intimate to any one, except Mr. Pomeroy (with
whom you may advise, you having imposed
the same injunction on him), from whence
the money proceeds, except that you may
say, when it is necessary to do so, that it is

sent to you from Massachusetts. Perhaps some one will appear, who will give money to build it up at once, but I know of no one. The building when completed should be a handsome one, and of stone or brick."

Two years later the development of the people and the heroic deaths of some of the young men of Kansas seemed to Mr. Lawrence to give both a reason and a name for a college, and he then wrote to Rev. Mr. Nute, of Lawrence, and Governor Robinson.

Boston, *December* 16, 1856.

Dear Sir, — Some time ago I requested Governor Robinson to spend some money for me in laying the foundation of a " preparatory school " in Lawrence, but the title to the land was imperfect, and the thing was not done. The plan of a preparatory department must be adopted before you can have a college; unless there should be a classical school established by the town. Nevertheless, I wish to see the plan adopted, and to help along its completion. I have thought it over much and it is briefly this, viz.: You shall have a college, which shall be a school of learning, and at the same time a monument to perpetuate the memory of

those martyrs of liberty who fell during
the recent struggle. Beneath it their dust
shall rest. In it shall burn the light of liberty, which shall never be extinguished till
it illumines the whole continent. It shall
be called the " Free State College," and all
the friends of freedom shall be invited to
lend it a helping hand.

Will you oblige me by conversing with
Governor Robinson in regard to this, and
with any other whom you would consult, but
without publicity. I cannot furnish cash
for building, but I can give what will be
as good for paying expenses after it is up.
For instance, having advanced $10,000 to
the university at Appleton, Wis., last year, I
hold their notes on interest. This is a good
institution, and owes little or nothing except
this. They have about two hundred thousand dollars' worth of property, and 450
students on their catalogue. I wish I had
money, but fear the time is distant when I
shall have more than enough to carry along
my plans begun long ago.

With great regard, yours truly,

A. A. L.

He thus wrote to Dr. Robinson: —

December 17, 1856.

Dear Sir, — . . . I wrote yesterday to Rev. Mr. Nute (with whom I had no personal acquaintance) about a monumental college, and requested him to consult with you. It is an old project of mine, and perhaps of yours. At any rate, I do not wish to lead off in it at all, and will not. It may seem assuming too much to suggest a name for it, but do so to prevent my own from being thought of, nor would I consent to it under any circumstances. It is a grand project, and I hope it will be carried out. It pains me not to be in a condition to take hold and put up the first building. . . .

Yours, A. A. L.

The immediate need of the State was not, however, a great monumental institution, but some educational system in all the towns and sparsely settled districts; therefore Mr. Lawrence wrote to Governor Geary: —

" To secure the adoption in all parts of the Territory of the best system of public schools seems to be desirable at this early day, and I have a plan to communicate to some one or two who have the leisure to attend to its execution. Some funds which I intended for the proposed university will be better used for the present for this purpose; and if the government should make adequate provisions for the former, no private contributions would be required. In the centre of this continent there should be a model State which shall be an example to all; a model for those which come in hereafter to copy, and a stimulant to the old States to keep up a high standard of learning, virtue, and patriotism."

Soon he placed in the hands of Dr. Robinson and Mr. S. C. Pomeroy, as trustees, $10,000 for educational purposes. The sum served as a stimulus to several religious bodies to organize educational institutions in order to obtain the income. In answer to an appeal from one denomination he wrote this letter : —

" The subject of denomination for the proposed college may turn out hereafter to be very important, and as it is decided now, so the institution may or may not be successful. But if it were left to myself to decide, I should be totally at a loss; and therefore it has appeared to be best to allow it to take its chance. Though a pretty rigid Episcopalian, I have no prejudice against any body of men who love the Lord Jesus Christ, and only hope that such men will control the affairs of the proposed seminary. The older we grow, the more we value simple piety, wherever we find it, and the less importance we attach to sects."

When the State University was founded in 1863, the $10,000 held by trustees in the city of Lawrence induced the government to place their university there, where it now forms a centre of literary life in that rapidly developing country.

VIII.

JOHN BROWN.

1855–1859.

THE other point of interest in Mr. Lawrence's Kansas experience is his relations to old John Brown of Harper's Ferry fame.

While John Brown was a wool merchant in 1843, Mr. Lawrence had made some purchases of him. When Brown's four sons, who were in Kansas, sent for their father to come out and help fight the border ruffians, he sought his old business acquaintance, who, as treasurer of the Emigrant Aid Company, was informed in Kansas matters. Mr. Lawrence gave him a letter to Dr. Robinson, and at the same time noted in his diary that "he had the look of a determined man."

The aim of the great body of Free State settlers who were led by Robinson was radically different from that of Brown. Theirs, as we have seen, was to create a free State by lawful means; his was to exterminate slavery with gun, pike, and sword. John Brown himself said to Dr. Robinson, that " the success in securing a free State was his failure ; " still, the opposition of the Free State party to the first elections of the territorial legislature brought them together for a time. Against the peaceful and constitutional measures of the Free State citizens Brown protested, and he soon entered on his course of violence and bloodshed, which, beginning at Pottawatomie, ended at Harper's Ferry.

In spite of the fact that Dr. Robinson wrote to Mr. Lawrence that Brown was "unreliable, and would as soon shoot a United States officer as a border ruffian," the excitement and violence of the times were such that deeds and methods were not tested with the nicety of sober judgment.

In January, 1857, John Brown came to Boston to testify before a legislative committee which had before it the subject of an appropriation of $100,000 for the aid of Kansas.

Mr. Lawrence's journal has this record : —

" January 6, 1857. Very cold and windy. Rode an hour and a half. Called at the United States Hotel on Captain John Brown, the old Kansas hero. Found Governor Robinson of Kansas at the Emigrant Aid rooms. Spent most of the forenoon with him. He has resigned his office, and the plan is to give Governor Geary, now a United States official, the popular vote, and so help on the ' Free State ' movement. Bought a fur coat for Robinson. Met Captain Brown; he is trying to raise a company to be ready in any emergency that may arise in Kansas. He looks a little thinner than when he went to Kansas with his sons. He fought the Missourians at Osawatomie in such a style as struck terror into the whole body of marauders. To Professor Longfellow's in Cambridge with my wife and Mary. A party mostly of young people. Played whist with Mr. Nathan Appleton, Mrs. Lothrop Motley, and Sarah. Home at half past ten, very cold. Deep drifts on the cross roads, Cambridge.

" 7. Very cold. Busy with Governor Robinson in forenoon. Captain John Brown, the old partisan hero of Kansas warfare, came to see me. I had a long talk with him. He is a calm, temperate, and pious man, but when roused he is a dreadful foe. He appears about sixty years old."

Friends of Brown were collecting money for him, and to them Mr. Lawrence wrote : —

Gentlemen, — Inclosed please find twenty-five dollars toward the fund for the brave Captain John Brown, who may appropriately be called the " Miles Standish " of Kansas. Few persons know the character of this man, or his services ; and he is the last one to proclaim his merits. His severe simplicity of habits, his determined energy, his heroic courage in the time of trial, all based on a deep religious faith, make him a true representative of the Puritanic warrior. I knew him before he went to Kansas, and have known more of him since, and should esteem the loss of his services, from poverty, or any other cause, almost irreparable. Perhaps there are those who would come forward and support his family while he gives his time to completing and keeping up the military organization of the Free State men. It would afford me pleasure to be one of ten, or a smaller number, to pay a thousand dollars per annum till the admission of Kansas into the Union, for this purpose. A. A. L.

The day after Brown's speech before the committee Mr. Lawrence inclosed seventy dollars to him, saying, "It is for your own personal use, and not for the cause in any other way than that."

Soon after, Mr. Lawrence received this letter written on the back of one of John Brown's "Circulars to the Friends of Freedom."

NEW HAVEN, CONN., *March* 11, 1857.

DEAR SIR, — The offer you so kindly made through the telegraph some time since emboldens me to propose the following for your consideration. For one thousand dollars cash I am offered an improved piece of land which with a little property I now have might enable my family, consisting of a wife and five minor children (the youngest not yet three years old), to procure a subsistence should I never return to them; my wife being a good economist, and a real old-fashioned business woman. She has gone through the two past winters in our open cold house, unfinished outside, and not plastered. I have no other income or means for their support. I have never hinted to any one else that I had a thought of asking for any help to provide in any such way for

my family, and should not to you, but for
your own suggestion. I fully believe I shall
get the help I need to operate with West.
Last night a private meeting of some gentlemen here voted to raise me one thousand
dollars in New Haven, for that purpose. If
you feel at all inclined to encourage me in
the measure I have proposed I shall be
grateful to get a line from you, care of
Massasoit House, Springfield, Mass.; and
will call when I come again to Boston. I
do not feel disposed to weary you with my
oft-repeated visitations. I believe I am indebted to you as the unknown giver of one
share of Emigrant Aid stock; as I can think
of no other so likely to have done it. Is my
appeal right?

Very respectfully your friend,
JOHN BROWN.

To this Mr. Lawrence answered: —

BOSTON, *March* 20, 1857.

MY DEAR SIR, — Your letter from New
Haven is received. I have just sent to Kansas nearly fourteen thousand dollars to establish a fund to be used: 1. To secure the
best system of common schools for Kansas
that exists in the country. 2. To establish
Sunday-schools.

The property is held by two trustees in Kansas, and cannot return to me. On this account, and because I am always short of money, I have not the cash to use for the purpose you name. But in case anything should occur while you are engaged in a good cause, to shorten your life, you may be assured that your wife and children shall be cared for more liberally than you now propose. The family of "Captain John Brown of Osawatomie" will not be turned out to starve in this country, until liberty herself is driven out.

Yours with regard,   A. A. L.

He immediately drew up this subscription paper and headed it with the names of his brother and himself : —

" The family of Captain John Brown of Osawatomie has no means of support, owing to the oppression to which he has been subjected in Kansas Territory. It is proposed to put them (his wife and five children) in possession of the means of supporting themselves as far as possible for persons in their situation. The undersigned, therefore, will pay the following sums, provided one thousand dollars shall be raised. With this sum a small farm can be now purchased in the neighborhood of their late residence in Essex County, New York."

But Brown was anxious to have his affairs settled and his family provided for, as his life was always in danger. So in a few days he sent this letter of urgency to Mr. Lawrence:

SPRINGFIELD, MASS., *April* 16, 1857.

DEAR SIR, — I expect to leave these parts within four or five days, and would be most grateful for the proceeds of the subscription you so generously started for me, so that I may effect the arrangement before I part with my family. I am sorry to burden you with any of my wants, but I must cast myself on those most kind. Please direct to John (not Captain) Brown, care of Massasoit House, Springfield, Mass. Please say to me what is the fate of the subscription at any rate, and greatly oblige your sincere friend.

Very respectfully yours,

JOHN BROWN.

After a few months the sum was made up with the aid of Mr. George L. Stearns and a few other friends of Brown and the farm at North Elba, where his widow lived for several years, was paid for.

In the mean time Brown had started for Kansas, followed by a letter from Mr. Lawrence to Governor Robinson, in which he said: "Old Brown (John Brown) will be your humble servant and an efficient one, but he requires some coaxing as well as some controlling power near him."

In this Mr. Lawrence reckoned without his host.

Two years later, May 28, 1859, Mr. Lawrence recorded in his journal, "Captain John Brown of Osawatomie called to see me with one of his rangers. He has been stealing negroes and running them off from Missouri. He has a monomania on that subject, I think, and would be hanged if he were taken in a slave State. He has allowed his beard to grow since I saw him last, which changes his appearance entirely, as it is almost white and very long. He and his companion both have the fever and ague, somewhat, probably a righteous visitation for their fanaticism."

In the following October the country, which was in a sensitive frame of mind, was startled by the news of the attack on Harper's Ferry and the attempt to arouse a slave insurrection; and then occurred the

trial of " Old Brown," who by his courage
and evident sincerity won the admiration of
millions who condemned his methods. The
journal of Mr. Lawrence at this time runs :

" October 18. The telegraph gives an account of an attempt at insurrection among
the negroes at Harper's Ferry under the
head of my Kansas acquaintance, 'Old Captain John Brown of Osawatomie.' The
old man has become a desperate abolitionist,
and hates the slaveholders the more because
he believes that they are responsible as a
class for the death of one of his sons and
the imprisonment and insanity of another."

" 21. Cold. Henry Wilson came to see
me about Brown. He thinks it will have a
very bad effect on the Republican party;
thinks all such attempts must fail always.
Brown's conversations are all given in the
newspapers by telegraph. He is a brave
man, and if he is hanged he will die a martyr to his hatred of slavery."

" 24. G. L. Stearns came at my request.
He told me that the rifles were the lot which
were turned over to ' Old Brown ' by the
National Committee ; he did not suppose that
they would be used for an insurrection, but
only to defend the Kansas settlers."

" 26.   Dr. Samuel G. Howe came to ask me if I would be one of ten to furnish good counsel to defend ' Old Brown,' to which I agreed."

" November 1.   The newspapers are full of Old Brown and his trial.   He carries himself wonderfully well.   He scorns the plea of insanity which was set up by his counsel."

" 5.   Old Brown convicted.   He made a brief speech that was worthy of the best of the early reformers.   To-day I was told that his wife was in Boston, and I went with Dr. Webb to the American House to see her. She appears well.   She is a large, strong woman, good-looking, and when young she must have been handsome.   She feels the loss of her two sons and the critical situation of her husband very much.   She says that it is a matter of religious conviction with her husband ; that he would make the same attempt again if set free.   I admire the old man ; but considering that three persons were killed by his party, I do not see how he can escape death, even had the occurrence been in a free State.   He will be lauded by the abolitionists as a martyred hero, and he does resemble that.   His death will hasten the removal of slaves from Virginia."

" 22. Rain-storm. The excitement in Virginia is very great; the fear of insurrection and all kinds of fear."

" 25. Looked over the report of the committee of Congress which went to Kansas in 1856 to investigate the troubles there. I did this in order to ascertain whether John Brown committed murder at Pottawatomie Creek in May, 1856. The affidavits show that a party which he commanded did take five men from their houses at night on the 24th of May, 1856, and murdered them at once. These were pro-slavery men, and they were killed when there was danger that the Missourians would get possession of the government of Kansas."

" 29. Great preparations for hanging Brown. Two thousand troops in barracks to prevent any attempt at rescue."

" December 3. Old Brown hanged with great ceremony. He died grandly. Nevertheless he must be called a fanatic. Declined to sign a call for expressing adherence to the Union, not being conscious that I have ever done or said anything to endanger the Union, and not wishing to certify my adherence to the Union very often for the benefit of politicians."

" 5. Declined to serve as vice-president of the Union meeting at Faneuil Hall, because I do not wish to help the Democrats.

" 6. Storm. Agreed to be at Faneuil Hall and act as an officer of the meeting. Public meeting at Faneuil Hall. A grand affair. The crowd was very great even on the outside. Ex-Governor Lincoln presided. Though over eighty years old he appeared well. Mr. Everett spoke as well as I ever heard him. Then Caleb Cushing. The enthusiasm was tremendous whenever the *Union* was alluded to. The Democrats will try to make something of it."

"11. Old John Brown was buried at North Elba in New York near his own house. A favorite tune of his was ' Blow ye the trumpet, blow.' This was sung by the neighbors."

On the second day of Brown's trial Mr. Lawrence wrote to Governor Wise of Virginia : —

Boston, October 26, 1859.

Dear Sir, — From the telegraphic report of the trial of Captain Brown it appears to be uncertain whether he will have a trial in the usual form. Permit one who loves the whole country as much as yourself to urge on you the necessity of securing this. Brown is a Puritan whose mind has become disordered by hardship and illness. He has the qualities which endear him to our people, and his sudden execution would send a thrill of horror through the whole North. From his blood would spring an army of martyrs, all eager to die in the cause of human liberty. I am sure that I express the desire of all conservative men here, when I beg you to insist on a fair trial.

Respectfully and truly,

Your obedient servant,

A. A. L.

Soon after the trial he wrote to Governor Robinson, "If they hang Old Brown, Virginia will be a free State sooner than they expect. He has played his part grandly, though the plot of the play is a poor one."

The evidence at his trial brought out the facts that Brown had been planning his raid for months, that money which had been given him for Kansas had been appropriated for this scheme, and that he had surreptitiously gained possession of the rifles which Mr. Lawrence had bought of the Sharps Company for use in Kansas, and which were at that time held in trust by the Kansas National Committee.

The result was that though Brown had confided his scheme to a few of his abolitionist friends, the Southern politicians had an opportunity, which they used with effect, of drawing into the affair the names of many men who had assisted Brown at other times.

On this account Mr. Lawrence wrote this letter to Senator Jefferson Davis : —

Boston, *December* 22, 1859.

DEAR SIR, — I am sorry to see, by a reported speech of yours, that you are among those who have been duped by vile fellows who believe that a large number of decent men in this part of the country are implicated in the affair of Harper's Ferry. Among other names I find my own, and I am the person alluded to as a cotton speculator who employed Brown to do his work. To show you how absurd this whole plan of libel will appear when it is examined, I will state my own case.

1st. I am the son of Amos Lawrence, now deceased, whom you knew, and who brought me up to be a " national " man, as

we understand that term.   2d. I have been
so decided in my own opposition to the formation of sectional parties, that those who
voted for Fillmore in Massachusetts, in
1856, nominated me for governor, but I declined. They have requested me to be a
candidate every year since that, and last
year I did run against Mr. Banks. 3d.
Though largely interested in cotton factories as a shareholder, I never owned a bale
of cotton in my life, and never had any business with any person whom I knew as a
speculator in cotton. Some years ago I
took a great interest in our people who settled in Kansas, many of whom went from
Lowell and Lawrence with their families.
They were shockingly abused, and if it were
not for my wife and seven children at home,
I would have taken a more active part in
that business. But that has passed long
ago ; it did not induce me to join the Republicans, though it did most of my friends.
I took part with Mr. William Appleton
and my relative Mr. F. Pierce in the Faneuil Hall meeting here the other day, and
with most of our people am called a "hun-
ker," and even in Mississippi should be a
law and order man. You will do me a

favor, if you will prevent my being summoned to Washington on so foolish an errand as to testify about Harper's Ferry.

Respectfully and truly yours,

A. A. L.

When in 1879 the confession of one of Brown's Pottawatomie party brought out into clearer light than ever before the brutal midnight attack on the Doyles and the almost savage methods of Brown's humanity, Mr. Lawrence became more firmly convinced in his early opinion that Brown's career was that of an earnest heroic spirit who, brooding over the wrongs of slavery and the death of his sons in the cause of freedom, had developed a monomania which regarded no law, provided only that his purpose was accomplished in his own way.

IX.

1856–1861.

His Kansas experience did not move Mr. Lawrence from his hunkerish sympathies in politics. He still felt that the great danger to the Union was the encouragement of sectional spirit. In criticising an anti-slavery resolve, he said: " By assuming that the honor and virtue and patriotism of the country are concentrated in the free States, or that these qualities largely preponderate here, we place ourselves in a position which we cannot maintain, and we cherish that sectional exclusiveness and that love of sectional power which is more dangerous to our national existence and to the true interests of liberty than anything else.

The elections of Sumner and then of Wilson to the Senate seemed to him little less than calamities. Though the trimming policy of the Whig Representatives in Congress gave him but little satisfaction, yet the Abolitionist and Republican policies were far more dangerous.

His patriotism led him to take an active interest in the strengthening of the conservative party, but he disliked to be drawn into political associations. " I can do nothing here," he wrote to a friend at Washington, " without going into state politics, a dirty pool, but not easy to keep out of always. The leaders of the American party are neither my friends nor acquaintances." But the fact that he was a conservative and had at the same time been so active in attacking the slave power in Kansas made him an available candidate for the party which was struggling in vain to hold the Whig and Republican elements together. The result was that, in 1856, he was nominated by the " Americans " for governor, although he had already declined the nomination of the Springfield Convention as a Frémont presidential elector.

Believing that his acceptance of the nomination from those parties would discourage his friends in Kansas, he felt justified in declining. It was just at this time that Mr. Sumner was recovering from the assault upon him by Brooks in the Senate, which sent such a shock through the country at what was considered a typical blow of slavery, brutal and cowardly. As the assault had been made on account of Mr. Sumner's speech on "The Crime against Kansas," Mr. Lawrence, in spite of his strong antipathy to Mr. Sumner's general policy, wrote this invitation : —

COTTAGE FARM, BROOKLINE, *October* 10, 1856.

MY DEAR SIR, — Having been informed that you contemplate making a visit to Boston, and knowing how difficult it will be for you to avoid the fatigue and excitement which must attend your stay within the city, I beg to offer you a home at my house.

You may prefer to be with some one of those who agree with you in regard to party politics, and you will without doubt have many invitations from nearer and dearer friends than I am ; but I assure you that no one will give you a more cordial welcome.

With much regard, yours truly,

A. A. L.

It seems hardly credible to-day that for this act of hospitality Mr. Lawrence met with criticism from politicians, and felt obliged to write to Professor Longfellow, "Mr. Sumner's speech on the 'Kansas Crime' alone entitles him to the gratitude of every man who has an American heart, whatever may be his politics. He will always have mine, and shall be welcome to my house as long as I have one."

The return of Mr. Sumner to Boston was accompanied by an enthusiasm that suggested a popular sympathy with him if not also with his political principles. Mr. Lawrence recalls the reception : —

"November 3. The newspapers advertise Mr. Sumner's reception to take place to-day: that he will be received by a committee at my house, thence taken to Boston, where he will be received at the Roxbury line by the Mayor and city authorities and a cavalcade of citizens, and an address to be made to him by Josiah Quincy, Sen. (eighty-six years old), thence to the state house, where he will be welcomed by the Governor.

"I went to Boston as usual. Came out at one. Found Mr. Sumner here, with Mr. Longfellow, Rev. Dr. Huntington, Dr. Perry, his physician, and his brother George.

"He lunched, conversed with a reporter for

the press, and gave him his speech in manuscript, after which I sent the reporter to town. He appears well when sitting, but is feeble when standing. I gave him a parlor to himself, and shut him up to avoid fatigue and enable him to prepare his speeches. He was here an hour and a half. I gave him some wine before starting, then delivered him over to the committee, who were in barouches. They had reserved a seat for me by the side of Mr. Sumner, but I declined to go. I thought the committee were disappointed, and also at seeing a Fillmore flag flying at the side of my house. But they had told me the reception was to be without distinction of party, and I took them on their own ground. After dinner I drove to town with Sarah and the children. Saw the procession from Mr. Appleton's. A long cavalcade, music, then carriages with Mr. Sumner and his friends."

Again in 1858 he was induced to lead a forlorn hope. He wrote to Governor Robinson of Kansas: —

July 24, 1858.

I am under the harrow again in regard to politics, and do not see any way of escape. If put up to run against Mr. Banks, I shall be beaten soundly. If for Congress, I might be successful; but it would be like cutting off my right hand to leave my wife and seven children (one recently), my business and all, to go to Washington. Without any desire to shirk the responsibility which every good citizen ought to be willing to assume, I am distressed beyond measure. If it were not for making myself ridiculous I would join the red-hot Republicans (who have many candidates) and so get rid of the difficulty.

In 1859 he would not allow his name to be used; but at the time of the great presidential election in 1860 he had, as four years before, thrown himself with great earnestness into the effort to unite the conservative elements of the different parties and to ward off the danger of disunion by the development of the National Union party. In March, his journal records, " For several days I have been very much occupied, having, in addition to my other pursuits, taken up the project of forming a party of conciliation in the country. ' Blessed are the peacemakers' is one of the promises. I have written a great many letters to influential men throughout the State, ex-governors and others, and have engaged in bringing together a convention on the 29th. Besides this, for several weeks I have employed agents to form 'Union' clubs in the towns and cities. It is a work of great labor, and I have no idea whether it will not appear a quixotic effort after all ; it certainly will be so regarded if it fails."

It took but a few weeks to show that the sentiment of Massachusetts had passed far beyond the platform of the Union party. But as the success of one of the other parties seemed to forebode disunion or war, loyalty to the Union kept a few thousand men together. Other candidates like Mr. Lawrence declined to be offered as a sacrifice, but at the convention he was pressed to yield his own preference, and after the nomination he went home, feeling, as he recorded in his journal, " better for having done my duty." The only other consolation that he received is found in the last sentence of this letter from his friend and classmate, E. Rockwood Hoar : —

Concord, September 13, 1860.

My dear Amos, — Considering, as you say, the state of the weather, the news from

Maine, and the prospects of your party, I admire your pluck.

I hope you will, some time or other before you die, belong to some respectable organization, having some definite principles, so that I can vote for you.

In the mean time, I congratulate your little squad on having a candidate who is neither "for sale or to let."

Very truly yours,
E. R. HOAR.

His strong political feeling did not affect his personal regard for others, for at the same time that he was working for the overthrow of Sumner's and Wilson's policy, he was writing to a fellow-member of the corporation of Harvard College that it was high time that Mr. Sumner be given the degree of LL. D., and he was also lending small sums of money to Mr. Wilson, who was as conscientious in the payment of his. smallest debts as he was honest in all his financial relations with the government.

During these years from 1856 to 1861 Mr. Lawrence followed the happy routine of his private and business life.

After removing to Longwood, in 1850, with two daughters and two sons, three more daughters were born, so that by 1858 the voices of seven children filled the house.

His position as president of the trustees of Groton Academy called him back at intervals to the old homestead, where in the barn, down at the meadow, or in the apple orchard and beside the cider press he renewed his old associations. He enjoyed nothing more than a call upon his old pensioner, "Uncle Oliver," whom he always kept supplied with tobacco, snuff, and other more useful though no better appreciated articles; or he would sit and talk for an hour or more in the cabin which he provided for the old negro nurse, "Peter," who used to sing his negro melodies to Mr. Lawrence when, as a motherless child, he lived upon the old farm. Writing to his aunt he said, "Good New England living ought to be encouraged by every head of a New England family, and at our house we always hope to have it. Apples and cider compose an important element. Of the last we crack 365 bottles in a year, and I only hope my children will drink nothing stronger during their lives. They surely can have nothing better."

His morning ride on horseback from Longwood to Boston, often covering eight miles about the country before getting to his office at nine o'clock, his return in the afternoon, and then a drive, a skate, or coast with the children, or a game of quoits with some of the neighbors, were his relaxations. A few extracts from his journals suggest the tenor of his life.

"January 4, 1858. Rode over to Jamaica Pond to see about skating. Found it good. Met the omnibus driver, Mr. Kemp, to whom I gave a hundred-dollar bank bill by mistake. Told him to give half of it to Duffy the blacksmith for the poor."

"April 19. Anniversary of the battle of Lexington. May God give us courage to defend the liberty of the institutions which our fathers have handed down to us."

"June 19. Last night a circumstance reminded me of the passage of years. At midnight I was awakened by vocal music from under the trees near my window. It was some Cambridge students. I could hardly realize that these young men have been born since I graduated. Poor Mary, for whom the serenade was intended, could not be awakened, for her door was locked.

" This afternoon we drove down upon the Western Avenue to see the regatta. The boys with me in my open wagon and the girls in the open carriage. 'The Harvard' beat in the large boat race."

" July 5. The boys came into my room as usual, when they were dressed, to say their prayers. I prayed with them and for them, that they might always love their country, and be ready to suffer and even to die in its defence."

" August 5. Atlantic telegraph laid and a message received. The whole country is electrified. Every assembly took notice of it. Thanksgivings offered by the clergy."

" October 22. In riding through Roxbury I saw immense placards calling on 'the friends of Amos A. Lawrence and Newell A. Thompson' to be present at a great ratification meeting this evening. Such things can do my name no good. I hope they will not result in any harm either to the name or to its owner. No one will suspect me of standing as a candidate this time in the expectation of getting into office."

" 28. Beautiful days. Up to top of Corey's Hill. Not a newspaper nor a public speaker has abused me. One of Mr. Banks's newspapers spoke of me in complimentary terms yesterday."

"December 13. Rode over to Jamaica Pond early, with my skates in my pocket. Tied my horse to a tree and skated half an hour on the most beautiful surface I ever saw. There was not a mark on the virgin ice, and as I flew over it I was reminded of 'angels' wings.' Reached town at nine.

"The Salmon Falls Company's account so bad that I have made an offer in writing to the directors through the treasurer to give up commissions enough to make the account up to three per cent. or $30,000."

"25. Christmas. Once more this delightful day returns, bringing with it the grateful memory of a Saviour's birth, and of his life on earth spent in poverty and suffering that He might bring to us salvation. There are the memories, too, of those who have been dear to us in this world, and who are now, as we trust, enjoying a better life in heaven.

"We had spent the evening with the children at Mr. Nathan Appleton's, where were about a hundred persons, young and old, relatives of the family and near friends. St. Nicholas (little Nathan) came in during the dancing, bringing a large basket on his back in which was a pretty present for every one of the young people. Then there was supper, and we returned to the parlors, where Mrs. Appleton arranged an old-fashioned contra-dance and invited me to be her partner, which I accepted. All this kept us up till quarter before eleven. But the children were awake in the morning not less early than usual, feeling for their stockings and admiring their presents.

"We went to Sunday-school and church. All were happy and I trust thankful. At five we went to town and dined at Mr. William Appleton's, where there was another gathering in the evening. At ten we left for home, bringing all at one trip, nine inside the carriage and myself riding as footman behind. If their precious lives are spared I would be content to ride always on the outside. May God bless them, and grant that they may never have cause to look back with sorrow on their present days of innocence."

"31. To-day my partnership with Mr. Mason is dissolved after about fifteen years. Walked to town against a driving snowstorm. Stopped at William's house; found him not very well. He is an invalid not

unfrequently, and sometimes I have anxiety
on his account. But I trust that he will be
spared to us. He is very dear to me, as an
only brother ought to be. This night, in
1852, my dear, good father went to heaven.
God grant that we may follow him whenever
our time on this earth shall be ended."

"1859. January 10. Cold. '14° below
zero at my house. Much colder elsewhere,
especially in New Hampshire and Vermont.
38 in Montpelier and in some other places.
Rode over to Cambridge. Asked a boy
about a poor woman who is dying of consumption. He knew her and told me she
had been burnt out (of the old Porter Tavern) and was living near. He jumped on
my horse and rode him up and down the road
while I went in and found the poor woman.
She was overjoyed at seeing me, and laughed
and cried by turns.

"11. Went over to see my poor woman
again."

" May 22. Sunday. Across the fields
with the children (how beautiful they are !)
to Sunday-school. With such company how
can any father wish for any situation in life
better than mine : how can any one have
more advantages than I have? Rev. Dr.

Stone preached two excellent sermons; and at sunset we enjoyed the sermon of nature in the golden colors of the sky.

"23. Rode up Corey's Hill. What a view! The country is clothed with verdure and with flowers; the trees covered with blossoms. The blessing of God seems to be present in such a fair scene."

"27. Cricket in the afternoon in my grove with the children."

"June 11. The spring is most beautiful. My horseback ride in the morning exhilarates me beyond anything which is not artificial excitement, and it is much more satisfactory than any art can produce. From Corey's Hill the view is wonderful."

"July 9. Solferino. Hell on this beautiful earth, and men turned into devils. God grant that the result may in some way conduce to extend his kingdom in this world of fallen men."

"19. Bought some 25-pound dumb-bells, as those which I have used are too light."

"December 27. Went to see F. E. Parker and asked him if he would be president of Harvard College if he were asked. He was very much surprised; said it seemed to him ridiculous, but was too serious to answer then.   I told him that I could vote for him confidently, and I believed Judge Hoar would, and his chance of election was as good as that of any one.

"28.   Parker declines."

"July 18, 1860.   Commencement.   At Cambridge at 8 in president's room.   Corporation there.   We tried on the President's new cap.   At ten we went to the library. Soon the Governor came with his aids, the overseers, etc.;   also Mr. Douglas, United States Senator.   Procession moved to church with a band of music.   On the platform were Messrs. Sumner, Wilson, Banks, Douglas, all men of mark.   My class mustered sixteen;   twenty-five years out of college.   Met in a room near the church; pleasing but sad remembrances.

"19.   Inauguration of president at Cambridge.   Heavy rain in morning.   Went to Cambridge in the saddle; got to Boston from there at half past nine, wet through. Home at two and changed dress, then to Cambridge again.   Went up in the pulpit where Mr. Felton was delivering his address with great earnestness.   The Governor and all the dignitaries of church and state, including ex-Presidents Everett, Quincy, and

Sparks. Mr. Quincy is quite feeble. I spoke to him afterwards and asked him if he was going to dinner with us, and he said ' No,' he was too feeble. I fear the old gentleman has taken part for the last time in the celebration of his Alma Mater.

" After the exercises in the church, we had the grand dinner in Harvard Hall; Henry Lee with his twenty marshals managing everything. I sat at the official table, next to Dr. Walton, the oldest graduate after Mr. Quincy; he is nearly ninety years old. Governor Banks spoke exceedingly well; so did Rev. Dr. Osgood. After satisfying my appetite, I went down and sat with my class."

" August 14. Up at five. Exercise with dumb-bells and in other ways. In afternoon went with Sarah and the two boys to Marion near Wareham, about two hours on the Old Colony Railroad. Found a good hotel. In the evening I danced a hornpipe with Judge Joel Parker, very much to the amusement of my good wife."

" 29. President Felton came after his return from Canada. He speaks well of the Prince of Wales; says he should think he might rank number twenty in a class of eighty if he should study for it; thinks he has been well trained."

"October 8. Two thousand citizens with torches and bands of music assembled from Boston and the neighboring towns and made me a visit in the evening. I stood in the doorway and received their salutes with my wife and children. I hope that the members of my family will not think more of this kind of applause than it is worth.

"26. A panic at the South about Lincoln's election. There is no cause for alarm from Mr. Lincoln, even if he had not against him both houses of Congress. The effort at the South for secession may produce anxiety, and they will not cease immediately after the election, if Lincoln should be chosen."

"November 7. Lincoln chosen president by immense majorities in almost all the free States. Breckinridge comes next in electoral votes; then Bell, and Douglas last. Andrew chosen governor of Massachusetts by an immense majority."

"29. Thanksgiving. Received notice to meet a town committee on Bradley's Hill, about buying it. Then went to church. Afterwards to see Henry Upham, who is unwell. The children went to James Amory's in the evening. The reminiscences grow too numerous to make such days cheerful ones, except as we should be cheerful in approaching the end of our journey."

" God bless my dear ones, and give them all grace to serve Thee all their days. Grant that we may all meet, when this life is over, in heaven.

" God bless my distracted country. Turn the hearts of the people toward each other again. Save us from disunion, and save us from shedding fraternal blood."

From 1857 to 1860 Mr. Lawrence was treasurer of Harvard College. It was an added duty which was undertaken out of loyalty to the college, and which yielded a good return in many pleasant associations with its officers and in a lengthened morning ride.

"1858. January 21. Over to Cambridge by arrangement with President Walker. Found him at breakfast (eight o'clock), rode round to the unfinished Appleton Chapel, where he soon met me and took me inside. There is no wood-work yet : nothing but the bare stone walls. He described to me the proposed arrangement of the interior, which I remarked as quite like an Episcopal church. He replied : ' There is such a thing as church architecture ; and as long as we have undertaken to build a church we may as well have a real one. It shall not belong to any sect. Here all sects must unite.' "

The magnetic spirit of Agassiz soon drew the interest of Mr. Lawrence towards the foundation of the museum.

" June 12. Professor Agassiz came to see me about his additional salary. He says he wishes to create the most complete collection of natural history in the world ; so that it shall command students not only from all parts of this country, but from Europe. I said to him, ' We shall draw students if we have the right man,' pointing to him. ' Yes,' he added, ' the man may draw students, but he cannot teach forever. He must go ; and then if you have not some other inducement, the students will go. It is such a collection of objects as I will make which will perpetuate the school.' He is a frank, hearty-looking man."

" November 17. President Walker, Chief Justice Shaw, Judge G. T. Bigelow, Rev.

Dr. Putnam, Professors Agassiz and Longfellow, Messrs. David Sears, W. Appleton, E. Rockwood Hoar, Jared Sparks, and J. A. Lowell dined here at four o'clock. They had an agreeable meeting. Chief Justice Shaw took Mrs. Lawrence in to dinner, though I asked Dr. Walker to do so; the former (who is seventy-eight) being more active than Dr. Walker, who is lame. The dinner was cooked by our own cook, Marion, and they all were cheerful and even gay; nor did they leave the dining - room until they went away. Mr. Agassiz sat next to me and talked all the time. I asked him whether some anecdotes about him in the newspapers to-day were true, but he had not seen them. . Then I repeated one about his replying to a person who offered him a large sum for some lectures, 'that he was too busy to waste his time in making money;' and this he pronounced to be true."

"January 21, 1859. Evening to James Lawrence's. Meeting of forty gentlemen about a building for Agassiz collection. Mr. Gray has given $50,000 for increasing and supporting the collection already made. Ex-Governor Clifford in the chair. Those who made remarks were Dr. Walker, Governor

Banks, ex-Governor Washburn, E. R. Hoar, Mr. George Ticknor, Dr. Gould, Dr. Jacob Bigelow, and myself. But Agassiz made the speech of the evening, very modest and characteristic ; all for the science, nothing for himself. Dr. Bigelow introduced a vote and called the collection the 'Agassiz Museum,' etc., but Agassiz interrupted him and declined decidedly. 'Personalities,' said he, 'must be banished from science.' "

" 26. Wednesday. Company to dinner at four. Agassiz, George Ticknor, Professor Felton, Rev. Dr. Huntington, Charles Hale (Speaker of House of Representatives), Lord Radstock, ex - Governor Washburn, and some gentlemen from the legislature whom I wished to become acquainted with Mr. Agassiz. They all seemed to have an agreeable visit, and I hope it will help along the project of establishing the Museum of Zoölogy at Cambridge. Lord Radstock is a young man, travelling with his wife."

"February 15. Subscribed $1,000 to Agassiz's museum in Cambridge. The committee now have $40,000 subscribed, and expect more."

"April 9. . . President Walker came to see about the Sanders donation. Before he left Mr. Agassiz came to get some money in advance ; and at the same time Governor Gardner came about something else."

" May 5. Meeting at my Court Street office of the committee appointed to be the faculty of the Agassiz Museum : President Walker, Dr. Jacob Bigelow, Dr. O. W. Holmes, and Mr. Agassiz. The latter is so progressive that it requires all the tact of Dr. Walker and Dr. Bigelow to keep him in check."

An interesting photograph of five presidents of Harvard College, now hanging in the college library, was taken under the following circumstances : —

" April 27, 1861. The President and ex-Presidents of Harvard College met at Whipple's by my request, to be photographed together for the college library. Messrs. Quincy, Everett, Sparks, Walker, and Felton. We waited for Mr. Everett, who had forgotten his appointment, and had a great deal of talk. Mr. Quincy was very bright and earnest. He told me he had enjoyed his life since he was seventy-four more than any previous part of it. He is now about ninety."

The pressure for charity continued at his

office, though, as he always remarked, it varied with the weather. His journal records: "December 11. Rainy. No beggars. Quiet day but busy in counting-room. 12. Fine day. Beggars plenty." For many years he made a standing offer to the agents of charitable societies that he would give a five-dollar gold piece to any poor person whose poverty was not caused by either drink, laziness, or bad temper. Experience and investigation assured him that there was no great risk in the offer. A more genteel class of beggars and money borrowers suggested these remarks : —

"August 1. Fine day. Annoyed by being forced to decline several applications for money. My experience leads me to know that the greater part of those who apply for loans or for gifts of money either live more expensively than their means warrant or they are unwilling to fix themselves down to one pursuit. If we should undertake to criticise cases, there would be found very few where hardship does not follow bad management and where relief can be anything but temporary."

It was a satisfaction to him to help raise a fund for Dr. Morton simply as his thank-offering for the " inestimable blessing of ether." In such a special emergency as the fall of the Pemberton Mills he was quick to join with others in carrying the paper about.

" 1860. January 10. Pemberton Mill at Lawrence fell down in one sudden ruin while in operation. The pay-roll shows 960 persons employed. While the multitude confined in the ruins were being dug out, a fire started and finished the horrible catastrophe.

" 11. Meeting of fifteen gentlemen at the Hospital Life office. We subscribed $2,000 on the spot for the sufferers. Meeting of the New England Societies in afternoon. Voted to omit the annual dinner to-day and added about $3,000 to the subscription.

" 12. Hard at work collecting money. Went with Beebe into State Street. All of us obtained $5,000 to-day."

In January, 1860, Mr. Lawrence took a short journey through the South with two nephews, and had the satisfaction of seeing Southern life near the end of the old régime.

" February 2. Savannah. Drove out two miles to an auction sale of 180 negroes. They looked serious, and the girls shed some tears. They were sold in families, and after they were knocked off I thought they looked anxious, and I noticed that a mother who was sold with her seven children sobbed very much. It is always a sad sight."

" 7. Negro dealing is carried on here by ' gentlemen ' of family who have been unfortunate in other business."

The travellers could see in the social life at the South no signs of the approaching outburst, for on arrival at home Mr. Lawrence wrote, " My neighbors think I must have incurred some risk in going to the South. How mistaken the opinion is of the two sections of the country in regard to the feelings of each other. May God make them more friendly and more emulous and excel in promoting the great cause for which our government was made."

The year 1860 closed under the shadow of the coming struggle.

" December 21. Laid up. Have worked too hard, and been too anxious for the Union. South Carolina secedes."

" December 24–30. This has been a week of anxious interest for the welfare of our country. Events follow in quick succession which will be felt in our future history for good or for evil, and I fear it will be the latter. The fear and hatred of the Republicans by the people of the South drives them forward to repudiate the government. In South Carolina the people have seized Fort Moultrie and Fort Pinckney and a United States cutter, besides the custom-house and other government property. They have now sent commissioners to Washington to treat for a partition of government property and to make a treaty with the United States. The President seems to be weak in supporting the government, and even leaning to the side of the traitors. Secretary Cass has resigned in disgust with the favor which is shown to nullification in the cabinet.

"Sunday. May the Lord spare us a little longer, and humble this great nation without inflicting us with the shedding of fraternal blood.

"31. Monday. A sad day. The anniversary of my dear father's death. A sad ending of one year in the history of my country; I fear the last year of our happy union."

X.

1861–1862.

FROM the special Fast Day of January 4, 1861, until the middle of April, national events moved with great rapidity, but popular sentiment moved faster. In spite of the increasing intensity of feeling between the North and the South, Congress was full of the talk of compromise and peace.

It was not in the nature of Mr. Lawrence, who loved peace and had an over-charitable confidence in the Southern loyalty to the Union, to let pass any consistent work for an amicable settlement. As one of a committee composed of Edward Everett, Robert C. Winthrop, and other representatives of the conservative elements of Massachusetts, he went to Washington with a petition of fifteen thousand citizens urging the passage by Congress of the Crittenden compromise. They were received by Mr. Buchanan, who, in dressing-gown and slippers, spoke with great anxiety in regard to a collision at the South, and expressed a strong desire (in which the whole North joined) to be free from the cares of office. They called upon Vice-President Breckinridge, General Scott, Mr. Seward, Mr. Sumner, and others, but the tide had set too strong for any such action. Mr. Sumner was too near the truth when he told the committee that their mission "would be of no more use than a penny whistle in a tempest." Having done his part for peace, Mr. Lawrence immediately prepared to do his part for war.

Two years before, in a speech on Washington's birthday, he had said, —

"It was a theory of Washington, and it has become the theory and the practice of this government, that the military power of the country shall reside in the people themselves; that, without a standing army, every citizen shall be accustomed to and shall be ready at all times to perform militia service.

"In accordance with this theory of Washington and our government, it becomes the duty of every citizen to have a knowledge of and to bear arms, and it is not hazarding too much to say that every citizen who has never

borne arms, and who has never submitted to
the military drill as commonly practised, has
not performed his whole duty, because he is
not ready at all times to perform any service
to which he may be called by his State or
Country."

Though he had taken his part as a young
man in the militia, he now felt that the test
of the principle had come. On his return
from Washington he threw himself with
great enthusiasm into the organization of
drill clubs. In February he wrote, "I go
to drill every day at eleven with about fifty
of various ages." In March he added,
"Drill club in afternoon; all in uniform
jackets and red caps; about ninety came out
and marched quietly to Boylston Hall (over
Boylston Market), where the exercise lasted
two hours. I do the whole with the youngest, because it is never too late to practise
what every citizen ought to be familiar with,
and because a good example stimulates others." Though twenty years older than most
of the men, his activity and endurance soon
made him an excellent drill-master. His
journal runs, April 17: "Find that I am
chosen quartermaster of our zouave regiment
proposed to be formed of Colonel Salignac's

drill club. Advertised to drill recruits to the number of 800."

At his invitation the zouaves would march out to Longwood and drill, while his family supplied barrels of lemonade. By comparison with later movements, those manœuvres had a very fresh and amateur appearance, but it was the first step in arousing the soldier spirit; and among those red-capped recruits were many who a few months later led battalions, regiments, and brigades into battle.

On the 15th of April came the proclamation of the President calling for 75,000 volunteers from the States, and the same day came a telegram to Governor Andrew to send forward 1,500 men. Popular feeling had moved on so rapidly that it was more than ready to respond. On hearing of the call for troops, Mr. Lawrence, who only a few weeks before had been urging Mr. Seward to act for peace, and who was still hopeful of some loyal sentiment in the South, now wrote him : —

Boston, *April* 1, 1861.

Dear Sir, — Permit a member of the Constitutional Union party to suggest that the call for 75,000 troops by the President will not have the desired effect on our friends in the South who are wavering about secession. If it were five times that number it would satisfy all that the government would be maintained, and I believe it would be responded to in the Northern States, and ultimately in the Border States.

Respectfully yours,

A. A. L.

Two weeks after he wrote to his friend, Henry Lee, of Governor Andrew's staff : —

Boston, *April* 17, 1861.

DEAR HENRY, — I don't wish to court notoriety by offering my service to Governor Andrew, but shall be glad to undertake any service of which I am capable. Therefore please to keep an eye out for me, where smart young chaps are wanted, and small pay.   Yours truly,

A. A. L.

His journal suggests the memories of that eventful week : —

"April 17. The Sixth Regiment muster in Boston, and march through the streets on their way to Washington, midst crowds of people.

"18. Troops going off to Washington in long trains of cars amid great enthusiasm."

"21. Monday. Great town meeting in Brookline. I made the committee's report, putting the whole town on the war footing, and appropriating $15,000 to be used by a military committee whom we named. This was adopted with great excitement.

"22. Thirty-five of my neighbors marched to Boston by way of drill. I led them part way, and then left them to Captain Wilder, as I was engaged at Cambridge. Great additions to drill club, over 400.

"23. Norfolk Navy Yard destroyed by government to prevent its being taken, with some of the finest ships of the navy.

"24. Drilling everywhere. To Brookline in evening. Drilled the townspeople; the halls filled.

"25. Massachusetts troops fired on in Baltimore. Washington barely saved from the revolutionists. Troops from the North sent through Annapolis. Arthur Lawrence in North Carolina. Mr. William Appleton in South Carolina.

"26. Railroad bridges all broken, north and west of Baltimore."

He added to his work as treasurer of the college one duty which gave him great delight. At eight o'clock in the morning he was in Cambridge drilling the students. His interest in them did not cease in the college yard, but followed many of them, his own young recruits, into camp, battle, and to death ; and his love for them and devotion to their memories prompted him, at the close of the war, to throw something of his old enthusiasm into the erection of the Memorial Hall. Not content with drilling townsmen and students, he gave the first lessons in the manual to his sons, and then sent them to Brookline to join a boys' company. In fact, as he wrote to his uncle, "We all drill, even my girls belong to a squad and carry arms well."

These were active days, as his journal testifies : —

"June 10. My daily duties sometimes press hard. First I rise and dress, say my own prayers, and prayers with some of my children. Before seven the triangle is struck for family prayers in the library. Breakfast at seven. Lay out work for men afterwards. Off on horseback at eight. Visit the contractors who are building for

me about here and the laborers on the
grounds. Then to Cambridge, oftenest to
look after new work or old — just now the
new house for president, and refitting the
Brattle House; or to meet the president
or steward or some one of the professors
on their business; or to review the college
'troops.' Then to Boston by half past nine.
Here are all sorts of business, commercial,
philanthropic, political; besides building of
three large stores, and a carriage factory,
and drilling my company daily. This pushes
me hard till after three, when I get on my
horse again and reach home a little late for
dinner. Then read the news, and rest until
I turn out to inspect my garden and workmen, or to take my wife to drive in my country wagon. All assemble at quarter before
eight o'clock at tea. Children's bed - time
and prayers with them at half past eight.
Then a nap, and reading or writing till
eleven or twelve. There is a great scarcity
of employment, and I have taken about thirty-five men to dig over my marshes, then to
haul gravel from them, then to cover with
loam, and sow grass seed."

"14. Drill in Pemberton Square. Very
hot."

His first thought was for the Union men in the border States, Tennessee and Kentucky. Those whom he knew he urged to adhere to the Union. To Senator Crittenden of Kentucky he wrote : " You can have but a faint idea of the indignation which has seized the people since the defeat of Anderson. Every man wishes to be a volunteer; business is suspended; political asperities have ceased, and we all stand as one man for the government. Our friends in Kentucky may rely on it, the government will be sustained and its seat will not be moved from Washington in our day. Why, then, should not they stand by it ? "

Andrew Johnson had written asking aid for the Union cause in Tennessee. Mr. Lawrence immediately sent $1,000, and started off among his friends with a subscription paper. It was an easy time for subscriptions. " Money is poured out like water. Thirty-three thousand dollars have been sent to my office in three days for the Massachusetts Soldiers' Fund. We are getting 100,000 men ready to go South in the fall, and when all our men have gone, then old Massachusetts is going herself."

The question as to whether a man in his

position with large financial responsibilities
as well as seven children should enter active
service was continually before him. In answer to a request of Mr. Paul Revere and
Dr. Coolidge, to take command of a regiment in which they were to be officers, he
wrote : —

Boston, *July* 3, 1861.

GENTLEMEN, — At a period like this, the
present duty of every loyal citizen will lead
him to abandon his occupations and his attachments for the public service whenever
those who have the appointing power demand it of him, but he is not to obtrude
himself into any position for which he is
unfitted, nor is he to urge his pretensions
for any position whatever.

With this view, I have carefully considered the proposition which you have been
kind enough to make to me, and have only
to say, that I shall always be ready to make
any sacrifice which the national or state
authorities may require of me. Though I
should have great diffidence in undertaking
military service, I stand ready to do anything
which others may decide I can do well.
Whatever it may be, I trust it will be undertaken simply as a duty, and without any

desire for notoriety or from any unworthy ambition.   Yours with regard,

A. A. L.

Again, in December, 1861, when Mr. Chase, the secretary of the treasury, was developing a plan for the movement to the Northern markets of those Southern staples that could be obtained, Mr. Lawrence wrote to him : " I have ventured to offer to devote myself to the government if I can render any service in perfecting the details of your plan. I will serve at any personal inconvenience and risk on any part of the Atlantic coast during the present winter, and longer if necessary, without any remuneration, except the payment of my expenses incurred in the transaction of the business. Having been a large buyer of cotton in Southern markets for manufacturing purposes, and a consigner of manufactured goods to those markets, and having had charge for many years of large numbers of free laborers of both sexes, in factory and in the field, I feel competent to do anything which can be done by any agent who would probably be solicited by the government."

Good service in the army he considered

as an equivalent for the payment of small debts, as is seen by this letter to a lieutenant in the field:—

DEAR SIR,— We cancel with pleasure our demand against you ($877.88) in consideration of your active services as a volunteer in supporting the government.
Yours truly,
MASON & LAWRENCE,
By A. A. L.

He offered a new house opposite his place in Longwood for invalid soldiers, and wrote: " I wish to offer my own services as steward, and those of my wife and family for any duties they can perform; promising that, if accepted, the routine of service shall be as faithfully performed as by regularly appointed agents; " adding, " In these times we are all desirous to do something for those who are fighting the battles, and for one I am desirous to be useful here rather than to leave a very large and young family for distant service. But if I cannot do one I shall feel bound to offer the other; though three years beyond the drafting age, I am strong and active, and can do anything required of younger men."

Another letter runs, " The Sanitary Commission may have the use of the store at the corner of West and Mason Streets free of rent, until further notice."

War meant death to the Whig and Union parties. When, then, the next canvass approached, Mr. Lawrence heard, to his surprise, that his name was to be joined with that of Governor Andrew on the Republican ticket. This compliment he declined, but from that time until the presidential election of 1886 he voted and worked with the Republican party.

At about this time the cruel treatment of our soldiers in Southern prisons had suggested the policy of retaliation in order to press the Southerners to humane methods. The kindly spirit of Mr. Lawrence suggested another policy. Having returned from a visit to the rebel prisoners at Fort Warren, he wrote to the commandant : —

" It probably has occurred to you that the treatment of the rebel prisoners will have an effect upon our own prisoners at the South.

" As the government rules are necessarily rigid, it is possible that the attentions of private citizens may be occupied in alleviating their condition in some measure. The loan of books, addition to their clothing, etc., may not come amiss to those who have been good citizens heretofore, and accustomed to the comforts of home. There is no doubt but that many of the soldiers were forced into the ranks in North Carolina, and I have supposed that some of the men who were more distinguished are held more as hostages than otherwise. It will afford me pleasure as a private citizen to assist in any plan which may require individual co-operation, though I do not suppose that it falls within your official duty to devise any such plan, unless to ascertain whether it is desired."

A letter to Mr. Robert Mason gives in a few words the drift of Mr. Lawrence's thoughts and feelings in 1862.

BOSTON, August 20, 1862.

DEAR ROBERT, — . . . The war now has reached very broad dimensions. With an army of a million, which we shall have (under pay at least) in November, and the new gunboats, the government will carry submission wherever it goes. Whether it will go into the interior of the South, except by gunboats, we cannot tell. It may be more expensive of life and money than profitable. The obstinacy of the rebels indicates that it will be necessary to ruin them completely and settle their lands with Yankees. The proclamation of emancipation of the slaves in the rebel States will be made whenever it will do more good than harm; and that time seems to be approaching. The President will not do it until the people of the loyal States are pretty much agreed upon it; and public opinion is setting that way more and more. The Yankee settlers in the South will get good day's work out of the negroes even if they are free.

The free States are very prosperous. Never have there been such crowds at the watering-places; never such an abundance of money. It may be like the days before the flood, when they ate and drank until Noah went into the ark, and the flood came and drowned them all. But so it is. There comes a heavy sorrow to many families after a great battle, and all the time there are bereavements which the public does not see. There were several funerals here at one time recently when the bodies of Captain Goodwin (Ozias's son), Captain Abbott (Judge Abbott's son), Captain Cary (T. G. Cary's son), Lieutenant Perkins (Stephen Perkins's son) were brought home. A son of Dr. Shurtleff was killed in the same engagement. One of Josiah Quincy's sons is missing; the time now elapsed makes it doubtful whether he is a prisoner. George Russell's son is a prisoner in close confinement; Quincy Shaw has been down there to learn about him, and his family have received two notes in pencil from him. These things make people feel rather sad; but they are small compared with the great mass of sorrow which all the deaths of soldiers create. But all does not have the effect of preventing our fashionable people from making fools of themselves, and of others. Down at Newport they say the balls are splendid.

Factory business better than ever, but looking forward into empty space. . . . Business is easily done; no dickering about prices; almost all sales for cash. Stores all shut up at two o'clock, when the bells begin to ring and the drums to beat. I wonder that any of the young men stay out of camp. I find it hard myself, though three years beyond the military age, and might be laughed at. Besides, it behooves every man to make sure that he is doing the best thing he can do, when he leaves a large family to go soldiering.   If he has a doubtful conscience he has made a blunder and will regret it all the time.   All well in my family.   They are at Swampscott for a few days longer.   Remember me to all yours, and regards to Mrs. Mason.   Yours very truly,

A. A. L.

XI.

THE WAR.

1862–1865.

THE summer campaign of 1862 had demonstrated to the government that the army was woefully weak in the cavalry service. Consequently in the autumn there was a strong movement by the government for additional mounted service.

Mr. Lawrence had been drilling with the sabre for some weeks, and had ridden and lived among horses from boyhood. This movement therefore seemed to give him an opportunity for more personal service than he had thus far given. He therefore wrote to Colonel Henry Lee of the governor's staff : —

BOSTON, October 5, 1862.

DEAR HARRY, — . . . Everybody wants to have a hand in putting an end to the war. If anybody who is authorized would direct me to recruit a regiment of cavalry for three years' service, I should think my time of service had come and should do my best to accomplish it.

Yours truly,   A. A. L.

The question whether he should himself enlist was settled by a letter from the Governor advising him against active service, and one from his friend, Major Gardiner, of the United States Army : —

"I would most strongly advise you against joining a cavalry regiment. I have been a cavalry officer for more than twenty years and know what the service is. No man is fitted for such service after thirty years unless he has been brought up to it, and even if he has been he ceases to be equal to it unless he is of an extraordinary constitution."

In answer to his letter to Colonel Lee, Mr. Lawrence received this letter from the Governor : —

COMMONWEALTH OF MASSACHUSETTS,
EXECUTIVE DEPARTMENT,
BOSTON, October 27, 1862.

SIR, — You are hereby authorized to recruit a battalion of four companies of cavalry (including the one coming from California) for three years or the war, and if

you can arrange with his honor, the Mayor
of Boston, to receive the city bounty upon
the remaining three hundred men, we shall
be ready, upon your assurances that they
will be forthcoming, to accept them as part
of the Boston quota.

Your obedient servant, etc.

JOHN A. ANDREW,

Governor, etc.

He had anticipated the formal authorization by writing to Captain Charles R. Lowell, who was at the time an aid to General
McClellan : —

BOSTON, *October 25, 1862.*

DEAR SIR, — I am authorized to assure
you that if you should think favorably of
the proposition to take command of a battalion of cavalry to be raised in this State
for three years' service, his excellency the
Governor will issue to you a commission of
major. In this case your presence will be
required here at once to assist in the organization of the battalion.

It is the intention to appoint captains who
are now in active service ; gentlemen with
whom you are probably acquainted.

Your obedient servant,   A. A. L.

The battalion soon developed into the Second Regiment of Cavalry, with Charles R. Lowell, colonel; Henry S. Russell, lieutenant-colonel; Caspar Crowninshield, major; and William H. Forbes, the son of Mr. John M. Forbes, who was associated with Mr. Lawrence in recruiting the regiment, as a captain.

The fascination of cavalry service and the reputation of its young colonel appealed to young men of good physique and active spirit, and soon applications came pouring in for commissions for their sons from mothers and fathers of young Harvard students and graduates, from ministers and Boston's dancing master, **Papanti.** It was an easy task to fill the list of officers. But the recruiting for the ranks was a different matter. The early days of the war had passed, when at town meetings and enthusiastic gatherings, after a stirring speech and roll of drums, the men had walked up to the platform and enlisted, amid the cheers of their neighbors and the tears of their families.

Massachusetts had sent over fifty thousand into the army and navy; drafts had been ordered, and " bounties " and " substitutes " were familiar words. The methods of recruiting in 1862 and 1863 were very business-like and not inspiring. Each town had its quota of men to fill. The recruiting agent, like Mr. Lawrence, would write to a town that he would supply them with men for their quota at the rate of $200 apiece. He would then send some officers of the regiment through the country or into Canada to raise men who for the bounty of from $100 to $175 would enlist — the remainder of the money going to the payment of expenses and the regimental fund.

At the time of recruiting the Second Cavalry, the farms, shops, and factories had been thoroughly ransacked, the army of bounty jumpers had developed, and even the jails had been called upon to open their gates to certain classes of prisoners, who on their promise to enlist were given their freedom. The result was that while there was a good body of patriotic young men in the ranks of the Second Cavalry, there was also a strong mixture of rough and mutinous elements, which, however, the firm and soldierly spirit of Lowell succeeded in disciplining. One day a squad of recruits in barracks showed an unruly spirit and the colonel was called. He found a serious mutiny in progress, and the men in the act of attacking their line officers with the sabre. Lowell drew his pistol and shot the ringleader dead, and then ordered the officers to march their men off for drill upon the common, thus removing them from the scene and keeping them occupied until the excitement was over. From that time the men learned that they had a commander to deal with. A company from California, composed largely of New England born men, came to Boston and swelled the ranks of the regiment. It was in the commonplace work of advertising for and receiving men that Mr. Lawrence's duty lay. But his pleasure was in the association with the young officers; and his counting-room often sounded with the click of the sabre as he taught some young lieutenant the first rudiments of the sabre manual.

In January, 1863, he was able to write to Governor Andrew : —

" It is now more than two months since you sent for me and gave an authorization to recruit a battalion of cavalry; and I am happy to inform your excellency that the duty has been performed. . . .

" There remains in my hands a considerable sum of money received from citizens and towns for the purpose of filling their quotas with three years' men. Of this an accurate account will be kept and the quotas will soon be filled as agreed. If any balance remains it will be turned over to the regiment; but if the sum should be insufficient, I shall cheerfully supply the deficiency."

On January 1, 1862, the Proclamation of Emancipation went into effect, and at about the same time came the movement for negro troops. On the 9th of February Mr. Lawrence received this letter: —

COUNCIL CHAMBER, *February* 9, 1863.

SIR, — I have invited the following gentlemen, with yourself, to act as a committee to advise and consult with myself and the officers of the regiment, in organizing and recruiting a colored regiment of volunteers, viz.: George L. Stearns, John M. Forbes, Dr. LeBaron Russell, Richard P. Hallowell, and Wm. I. Bowditch, with F. G. Shaw, Esq., of New York and Morris L. Hallowell of Philadelphia as corresponding members. I hope that you may be able to act upon this committee, and am

Very respectfully,

Your obedient servant,

JOHN A. ANDREW.

On the 28th of May the 54th Regiment, the first full colored regiment in the country, marched on to Boston Common. Colonel Robert G. Shaw, whom Mr. Lawrence describes as "youthful, handsome, sensible, determined, a model for a hero," marched at their head. The journal runs: —

"All Boston turned out to see the first regiment of negroes that had ever been raised in the Northern States. The officers are all educated gentlemen, and Shaw rode with Lieutenant-Colonel Hallowell (whose arm was still in a sling) at the head of the column. He was splendid. I stationed myself outside the window on a projection of one of the stone stores in Franklin Street, and as they came up with the bands playing and the people cheering from the street, and from the houses, with the flags flaunting, it was indeed a grand and novel sight. The troops marched beautifully. When Shaw and his staff came opposite I hailed him and bid him adieu. He raised his hat to me, and waved it toward me twice, at the same time speaking to Hallowell, who did the same. May God bless these dear youths. May God save our country from its foes. May God help this government to crush rebellion, and to crush its cause with it — slavery. Would to God, would to God, I could fight these battles for these young men."

In everything that related to himself and his home during these years, life ran smoothly, as the following letter testifies : —

LONGWOOD, *July* 31, 1863.

DEAR WIFE, — This day brings me up to forty-nine years. What a level plain of prosperity has my journey been across thus far ! Family, friends, fortune, all twining around, so that they alone seem to be a sufficient support. Yet it is plain that the time is not far off when they all will fail. May the grace of God strengthen me now, and then ; and save me from falling when the time of trial comes.   Yours affectionately,

A. A. LAWRENCE.

But the increase of blessings only added to the intensity of his sympathy for others less fortunate, especially when war had cut off the pride of a family.

He wrote to his cousin, whose nephew had met a noble death : —

(Near) Boston, *March* 11, 1864.

My dear Cousin Sallie,— The account of young Dahlgren's death reads like an ancient romance. How sad! how brilliant! how wonderful! What devotion! what intrepidity! what patriotism!

I recalled the appearance of the pale, maimed youth who sat on your piazza on the day of Abbott's funeral; when I pressed his hand and he mine as though we were blood relations, though we had never seen each other before. How he could have gained strength to ride on one of those painful, exhausting raids surpasses comprehension. But there he was, fighting like a hero; dying like a martyr; his body stripped and insulted and ignominiously buried. His memory will live when we are all dead and forgotten. May God's grace sustain his parents and his family under this great and sad, but hallowed affliction.

My tears drop right down while reading the extracts from the Richmond papers, — tears of sorrow, of anger, of joy that my country has produced such a noble youth, and that she has more.

I hope that you are well, and that life wears a brighter aspect for you. You are still young, and you may have many years of useful happiness.

We are all well at " Cottage Farm," including Henry A. Green's family. My Mary is looking forward to be married before summer. My wife sends her love.

Your affectionate cousin,

A. A. L.

A few extracts from his journal suggest the memory of those days.

" 1864. May 8. Sunday. All sorts of rumors, after service this afternoon. I saddled my horse and rode to Boston to learn the truth. Severe fighting, but no great victory. Eight thousand wounded and sent to the rear of Meade's army, and the first battle-ground in possession of our army. Spare us, O God, from defeat. Give us the victory. Give us peace."

"10. Severe fighting. Brigadier-General Wadsworth killed. Colonel Griswold of the Massachusetts 56th, the only child of a widow who lives near to us, is killed; also Major Abbott, son of Judge Josiah G. Abbott of Boston; this is the second son killed in battle in this war; he was in command of the Massachusetts 20th, and a very fine young officer.

"11.   The battle still raging in Virginia. Grant gains ground.   Major-General Sedgwick killed.   May God give us the victory, and confound the enemy.

" May 12.   Mary's wedding. . . .

" I could not stay at home without hearing from the army.   So I rode to Boston to learn the news, and afterwards rode to Waban Hill Farm.

" The fighting continues.   Very bloody, very desperate at times.   General Stevenson of Boston killed ; a good officer.   May the Lord of Hosts give our brave army the victory.   He alone can do it."

" June 21.   Wounded men are seen everywhere ; in the streets, on the railroad cars, at the railroad station.   Some badly maimed. Certainly there were never so many maimed men of one nation before, and the graves ! And the sorrowing hearts !   O God, how long ? "

" 24.   Cotton has sold at 165 cents a pound for ' middling '; and gold at 225 cents for a dollar.   Heavy sheetings about 60 cents a yard.   Cocheco prints at 37½ cents."

" 26.   Hot.   To church twice. How hard to bear is this oppressive heat by the poor fellows in the hospitals, and in the field. The great reaper, Death, has an abundant harvest. O God, listen to the prayers of the suffering people, and pardon our sins, and bless us once more."

" July 17. Philip Mason died at S. Hooper's house in Washington after great suffering. His thigh and part of one hand were shot away. Goodwin Stone of the Second Cavalry (Massachusetts) is mortally wounded. He was a young man of fine talent; one of the highest scholars at Cambridge of the class of '62. I obtained his commission for him, and gave him lessons in the broadsword exercise. His family live in Newburyport, and he was their pride; respected everywhere.

" We moved to Nahant, to our new house on the rocks, and are all well pleased with it. The addition which I have made to it has a good piazza all around on both stories; and the sea view is excellent."

" 23. Took tea at Mr. Longfellow's with Charles Sumner. The latter wishes to see a president with brains; one who can make a plan and carry it out."

" 25. The fighting in Georgia was severe. Not less than 6,000 rebels killed and wounded. Mr. Sumner thinks McPherson was fit to be placed at the head of the army.

"31. To-day I am fifty years old.

"It is not often that I think of my dear mother, whose image I cannot recall. Yet now I do bring up circumstances transpiring fifty years ago, when she first looked in tenderness on me. Can it be that she has been watching me since that time? And will she welcome me when God calls me home?"

"August 2. Salmon P. Chase (ex-Secretary of the Treasury), Agassiz, J. W. Paige, Horace Gray, S. Hooper, and myself made the company at dinner at Samuel T. Dana's, who lives on the north side of Nahant in Edward Motley's cottage.

"I asked Mr. Agassiz why no report was made by the late C. C. Felton, himself, and Benjamin Peirce, who were chosen a committee to investigate the subject of modern 'spiritualism.' He said the facts were too bad to publish; they implicated many most respectable persons ; and they would not be believed. The whole system only indicated how weak is human nature in resisting imposture, and in curbing the natural lusts of the flesh."

With the news of cavalry successes in

the autumn of 1864 came also the tidings of heavy losses from among the best men in the service. Mr. Lawrence followed every movement of the Second Cavalry with intense interest. It was therefore with a sharp pang of sorrow that he recorded the death of the young colonel whom only a few months before he had named to Governor Andrew as a soldier fit to command.

" October 24. Colonel Lowell's death confirmed. He was a splendid officer; a young man of fine talents and character, of great energy and of great accomplishments; the first scholar in Cambridge, and everywhere the first in action."

" 28. Colonel Charles R. Lowell's funeral at the college chapel in Cambridge. It was very impressive. The Cadets performed escort duty. He was the only son of his parents, his younger brother having been killed in Virginia in the Peninsular Campaign."

On the same day Mr. Lawrence wrote for the paper this notice of his death.

A GLORIOUS DEATH.

" The brigade of cavalry which was raised for General Buford is called the finest in the army.   After his death the command was assigned to Colonel Lowell, as a compliment to his services, and he acquitted himself in it so as to command the admiration of the officers and men.   General Sheridan was so struck with his efficiency that he urged the President to make him a brigadier-general, and the commission had been issued.   He had always exposed himself whenever he could render any service, leading his men, and fighting often like a private soldier. But in this campaign of thirty days his exposure had been very great; twelve horses had fallen under him, one of them struck in seven places, and his clothes had been riddled with balls; yet he had not been touched.

" His first wound was received about one o'clock on the day of the battle of Cedar Creek, from a spent ball which struck him in the breast.   The concussion of the lungs was so great as to cause anxiety.   General Torbett urged that he should be carried from the field ; but this he resisted.   Though his voice could only be raised to a whisper, ' he hoped to lead in the final charge ' : and so he did.   He was carried to the rear, and a little parapet of earth thrown up to shield him ; and he lay there motionless for two hours, having exacted a promise that he should be told when the charge was ordered. This came at three o'clock. He was then raised up and placed upon his horse, and for a time seemed to receive new life. He rode to the front, amid the cheers of the men, and took the command, which had devolved upon Lieutenant-Colonel Caspar Crownin-shield. His clear voice was gone, but all saw by the waving of his sword and by his eye, what he meant. He whispered the orders to his officers and they were passed along the lines.

"It was half an hour before the bugle sounded the grand charge. Then his strength rose with the occasion : he threw into it his whole life : it was to him 'the final charge,' and to many other brave men. A ball pierced him from shoulder to shoulder, and, laid on a shelter tent, he was carried from the field. Though paralyzed, he remained conscious, and gave minute directions about the business of his command. He dictated letters and sent loving messages to his young wife, his parents, and friends, and, having finished all, he lay quietly expecting death. No doubt he was prepared

for it, for the whole of his brief life had
been spent in the performance of his duty.
Few men have combined so many talents
and accomplishments, so much learning and
so much virtue, with so strong a love of
country."

During the canvas of 1864 Mr. August
Belmont of New York wrote to the "New
York Times," offering to bet in the form of
two propositions of $10,000 each. The first
proposition was "that if Mr. Lincoln should
be elected, we will be in a state of war during the term of his administration or will
be forced to a disgraceful peace, with sepa-
ration." This drew from Mr. Lawrence,
whose admiration for the policy and character of Mr. Lincoln led him for the first time
to vote for a Republican president, the following letter to the editor of the "Times."

(Near) BOSTON, *November* 4, 1864.

DEAR SIR, — The proposition of Mr.
Belmont in your paper of yesterday seems
to be calculated to influence doubting or
timid persons to vote with him. If you
think so, and if none of your people will
take him up on his first proposition, then I

will do it, provided the money shall be given to some charitable object in New York or Boston, at the option of the winner.

I have always voted against the Republican candidates, and never have bet, and have no money to spare at this time. I pray for peace as devoutly as Mr. Belmont, and for union, and believe that we shall have both, but not in the way he proposes.

Your obedient servant,
AMOS A. LAWRENCE.

Nothing was heard from Mr. Belmont.

The year 1864 closed with the news that the Confederacy had been cut in halves by Sherman's march.

"December 15. General Sherman's guns heard on the seaboard at Beaufort. Frank Lawrence at Port Royal writes, ' We hear the guns and hope to see Arthur soon." (Arthur is with Sherman.) This will be the greatest march of the war, if he gets through safely from the Mississippi to the sea."

"31. 11 P. M. My God, my Father. I would utter grateful thanks for the constant and unnumbered blessings on myself and on my family during the year just passing away. Lift up our hearts from the devoted love of this world to the love of thyself. Turn our eyes away from the contemplation of vain things upon our Saviour who suffered for us. Make us like Him. Accept our poor efforts; pardon our infirmities and sins; and prepare us for the great change that awaits us all, and finally receive us into thy heavenly kingdom. I ask this in the name of our dear Saviour, Jesus Christ; and for His sake, grant my prayer, O my God."

The year 1865 opened upon the final events of the Rebellion, when the rapid succession of victorious news was eclipsed by the tragic week in April.

" April 2. Major Charles H. Mills of Boston killed. He had been at home for a long time badly wounded, and we had seen him about the streets and in company repeatedly; in fact he had only just left us for ' the front ' when he was cut down in the flower of his youth. O God, give us peace; peace with good government; peace with liberty. This is Sunday. How sad to many hearts all over the land.

" 3. *Richmond surrendered.* Thanks be to Almighty God.

" 4. Great rejoicing, and no business done."

" 6.   I am building a new library on the
south side of my house, and in the stone at
the base of the chimney outside, I have had
an inscription cut, ' RICH. VICT. APR. III.
A. D. MDCCCLXV.' "

" 9.   General Lee's army surrendered to
General Grant. Thanks be to Almighty
God for this. Now He smiles once more
upon us.   I have ordered another inscription cut in the stone of my ' Memorial
room ' as I propose to call it. ' EXERCIT.
CONFED. DEDITUS. APR. IX. MDCCCLXV.'

" 10.   Rejoicing, flags, cannon firing, fire
works, illuminations and thanksgiving, and
little else."

" 15.   President   Lincoln   assassinated.
While we were at breakfast the waiting-
maid came in and said that President Lincoln and Mr. Seward were assassinated.
At that moment the Brookline bell struck
and the town flag was hoisted to half-mast.
This told the story. The news had just
come, in fact the President had but just then
died. This shows the wickedness of the Rebellion and the desperation of the rebels.   I
ordered a new inscription to be cut: ' POP.
GAUDIO SUCCEDIT SUMMUS DOLOR. APR.
XIV. MDCCCLXV.' All the bells over the

whole country are tolling; all the flags at half-mast. Mourning everywhere.

"16. Mourning everywhere for Mr. Lincoln. (Mr. Seward and his son not dead, but very ill from wounds.) The houses all draped more or less with black and white, and all the stores.

"17. Put one more inscription in the stone. 'SICUT PATRIBUS SIT DEUS NOBIS.'"

"June 1. Grand procession of mourning for Mr. Lincoln. This day is appointed by the President as a day of mourning. In the morning at 9 A. M. we went to church. The display of military was large, commanded by General Bartlett, 'the bravest of the brave,' who rides as well as though he had as many legs and arms as he had before the war. Many officers and men scarred and browned with their campaigns were in the procession; but as interesting as any were the great vans filled with soldiers who had lost their lower limbs and who could not walk. These were cheered more than any."

To Mr. Mason he wrote : —

BOSTON, *June* 28, 1865.

DEAR ROBERT, — The regiments are

coming home fast. Every day we see the swarthy veterans marching through the streets. The railroad stations, the cars, everything is alive with them. Just now the 4th Massachusetts Artillery is passing up the street. The colonel (King) has been knocked pretty much to pieces; but he sits erect on his horse and looks as handsome as ever, though his hair has turned to gray. Several officers have only one arm or have lost a leg. The drum major is a perfect giant. The men are very thin and the color of Spaniards; they look straight forward, and do not mind the cheering. At every step some relative or friend recognizes a soldier and calls him by name, which causes him to look in that direction. Then as the rusty flag passes, everybody gives it a cheer. This is going on all over the country. The officers put on their civilian dress the next day after they are mustered out, and the men take off their buttons and faded trimmings at once, so that in a few weeks we shall see no soldiers.

The year 1865 closed with the final war scene.

"December 22. Forefathers' Day. A

procession of all the regiments which have been to the war, with all their flags. These last they carried to the state house and delivered to the Governor. It was a touching sight. Most of the regiments were represented by a score or two of men, with their colonel in most cases at their head. Some had as many as one hundred. Some had one old, tattered, faded flag. Some had several. The men had but little uniform. Being disbanded, they had gone to their old pursuits, and had no uniform, except a few. Some were wounded, one poor fellow had lost both arms. There were over sixty regiments in all, and when all the flags had been taken by the Governor they were displayed in front of the state house. That was a glorious sight as it was seen from the Common. Many a poor wounded and dying soldier had looked on one or another of these flags, now displayed to an admiring throng of his fellow countrymen who enjoy what he gave his life to obtain, a good, stable government."

XII.

It was a favorite idea with Mr. Lawrence that after a man had passed the age of forty his gain in. wisdom and experience did not counterbalance the loss in activity of mind and body and the gradual failure of the executive faculty. On this principle he was always an advocate of putting young men of promise into responsible executive positions; and he had that appreciation of the worth and intelligence of young men that under his guidance their best qualities were developed and their activities brought to the highest pressure. But the application of the principle to himself had this drawback, that when, at the close of the war, he had reached the age of fifty, he began to feel that his best years had passed and sometimes to affect an old age which really had no place in his strong physique. Having moved much with older men in his early business day, he looked upon them as his contemporaries, and whenever an acquaintance died who was not more than twenty or thirty years older than himself, he felt that one of his own age had departed and that his own time must soon come. With a man of his intense activity and nervous temperament, reactions were sure to occur, and at this time we begin to read the first note of what later became sometimes a rather melancholy strain. Anniversaries suggested sad rather than hopeful thoughts.

"July 31. My birthday. My life seems to be passing away without any great result. My chief care and ambition for this world now centres in the welfare of my children. Age makes me less sanguine about changing the destinies of men, and I cease to take an active part in popular movements. God give grace to save me from a sordid selfish ease."

"August 7. Since the war and since so many of my friends have gone abroad, I look too much on the dark side. Ambition seems to have died out and great hopes have ceased to be excited."

The following letter to his Uncle Giles Richards suggests the double life which intensified as he grew older, — that of an introspective melancholy bound to an earnest faith, which was so common among our New England ancestors, combined with a vivacity and cheerfulness in society of which our fathers were seldom guilty.

December 7, 1865. Thanksgiving Evening.

MY DEAR UNCLE, — On these anniversary days the memory runs back to the days long passed away, and it requires a great effort for any except the very young to avoid an overpowering feeling of sadness. I think of you in what was not many years ago your " new home," surrounded with all that makes life sweet. The glad voices of your children, the tender smile of their mother, all united to warm your heart and to make you thank God for so much happiness.

Now in your " old home " you sit by your hearth, an old man, the lamp growing dim, the bright lights of former days gone out. The forms so dear are not seen; their cheerful voices are not heard. Yet in your own imagination you do see them, and you do hear their voices. But their forms are more heavenly, and their voices are calling on you to prepare to rejoin them. No doubt you will gladly obey the summons when in God's good time it shall come. Meantime you will live for those who remain to you, cheerful and cheering, in the service of the Lord, and in communion with his saints.

All this reminds me of my own life, so filled with blessing, yet fast gliding away. All my dear ones remain with me. My good wife, seven children, and one grandchild, all are here under this roof. I see their forms, to me the most beautiful on earth, and I hear their voices on this Thanksgiving evening. Indeed, I have cause for thankfulness, though the black clouds of sorrow should gather from this very hour; still I could be thankful, for my cup of blessing has long been full and running over. Who that has lived fifty years can enjoy these family days without some sadness, if those cannot who have been prospered all the time.

Sunday 10th. My note was stopped by the influx of some twenty young people, chiefly nephews and nieces, who assembled here to have " high jinks " on Thanksgiving evening. There were two families of Uncle William L.'s grandchildren (Sprague and Whitney), two families of Uncle Abbott's grandchildren (Abbott L.'s and Rotch), and

an equal number of Appleton grandchildren.
They soon had possession of my sanctum
where this is written, and turned me out to
help play the "elephant," to "wind the
bottle," to see "the dwarf" and the "giant." The sport ran high from six o'clock
till nine, and then they disappeared into the
snow-storm to their homes. They like to
come to Uncle Amos's; they think, no doubt,
that I have been here always, and that I am
as lasting as the hills. If the new heaven
and the new earth are to be our everlasting
home, then in our human weakness some
might pray that this present home may be
ours hereafter. Certainly I should be one
to ask to live right here.

Your affectionate nephew,

A. A. L.

None of this inner melancholy tone was
noticeable to his friends, however, except that
he occasionally "talked old," and heard with
satisfaction mingled with chagrin that some
one had taken him for an old man. In fact
his bald head, encircled by the finest silken
hair, which was too silvery to turn gray,
gave him that appearance. But his strong,
stocky, active body, smooth complexion, soft

skin, and clear blue eye were certain marks that great vigor still remained. And his habits were those of a vigorous man. A few minutes' exercise before the open window with his twenty-five-pound dumb-bells preceded breakfast, at which he was sure to find his whole family, his wife and seven children, promptly at seven o'clock. In those years Longwood had only candles to dispel the wintry gloom from the breakfast-room. At quarter before eight family prayers were over and his horse, which was often an ugly-tempered, ill-trained, or high-strung beast, was at the door. He was then off for the country — sometimes to rap with his whip on the window of his pastor, Dr. Stone, or his loved friend and relative, James S. Amory, or to rouse from the breakfast-table some other neighbor.

While treasurer of the college he usually took Cambridge into his circuit. After 1862 his farm at Waban Hill in Newton always received one visit in the day. But, a few minutes after nine he had thrown the rein on his horse's neck in the stable in Mason Street at the rear of his father's house, and was on his way to the counting-room at 17 Milk Street. (In 1869 he

"50 years of horseback".

removed his office to 13 Chauncy Street.) Six hours of active business, including the reception of beggars, borrowers, and acquaintances with schemes to unfold, gave him the impulse for a sharp ride home over the Mill-dam. Dinner and a five minutes' nap refreshed him for a drive, a skate on Jamaica Pond, or another ride on a fresh horse, from which he returned after dark ready for his tea, newspaper, and pipe or cigar. This life on the road made him a familiar figure, and that person was a stranger in Brookline who did not recognize and give a passing nod to Mr. Lawrence. For his taste was so social that he was ready to stop and have a chat with any one. Every workman on the road looked up with the feeling that he would be recognized and accosted, and it was seldom that Mr. Lawrence did not carry away from his conversation a piece of useful information, while the Irishman retained a kindly feeling and often a gold dollar for the children; for Mr. Lawrence always carried gold to give away even in the days of its highest premium. Duffy, the blacksmith, was the means of quietly passing from five to fifty dollars into the hands of his neighbors.

And for the mechanics and tradesmen in the town he had as respectful and neighborly interest as he did for his friends Dr. Francis, Dr. Wharton, or Mr. Winthrop.

It was this perfectly natural sympathy with men of all sorts, combined with his other conditions, that gave him a unique position in the community. At the town meetings, though he was not a ready speaker, he had that business-like but kindly manner, mixed with a little dry wit, which disarmed criticism, created confidence, and sent a glow of kindly feeling among those who were wrangling about some great questions as the widening of a street or the draining of a marsh, such as rouse the passions of fellow townsmen. He never had the time to accept many long term offices in the town, but if there were any special question or new undertaking he was ready to take his share of the work. There was one kind of town improvement in which he always had an interest, — the laying out of play-grounds for the boys. His faith in the worth of physical exercise led him to join with others in creating a skating pond on the Aspinwall meadows, and building a floating bath-house on Charles River. And no part of his work in connection with the college interested him more than the building of the gymnasium and the purchase of Jarvis Field to take the place of the Delta, on which Memorial Hall was to be built.

Associated with his out-of-door life was his interest in adding to the beauty· of the towns, not only by parks but in the simpler way of creating in the people a pride in the neatness and beauty of their surroundings.

The meeting - house, the roads, and the cemetery at Groton were special objects of his care.

The following instances of the correction of public annoyances are mentioned not for their importance but simply as characteristic of the man. While the newspapers were scolding about the disfigurement of the towns and country by advertisements and posters, Mr. Lawrence was having copies of the stringent statutes on the subject mailed to the chief of police or selectmen in every town and village in the State, with an urgent request that the law be enforced. And it was a satisfaction to him to know that, largely through his influence, the two towns in which he lived permitted no advertisements or posters within their limits. It pleased him very much to try without success to induce a man with posters on the Cambridge side of Charles River to bring his advertisements across the line to Brookline.

The shriek of the Worcester Railroad whistle, as the trains shot across the crowded streets towards Boston, induced his brother and himself to offer through the " Daily Advertiser " the sum of " $10,000 to be given to the inventor of a system of signals in lieu of whistles." Whatever effect the offer may have had, their urgency of the matter upon the railroad officials resulted in causing the engineers to cease whistling several miles outside of Boston.

From the first day that he moved to Longwood, in 1851, he joined with his brother in laying out their tract of land, planting trees, opening up roads, and building houses; so that within a few years the Cottage Farm was covered with a cluster of stone and brick cottages which, hidden behind trees and hedges, gave it the appearance of a private park. And as the first object was the creation of a pleasant neighborhood, the houses were always filled with families who joined with each other in making a delightful and refined community.

In 1862 Mr. Lawrence anticipated the approach of Boston, which is now converting Cottage Farm into city streets, and bought a farm of over 100 acres about three miles farther out of town, on a part of the tract formerly occupied by the chief Waban and his tribe. It was an unrealized dream that he might retire to Waban Farm as Boston approached Longwood. But the city soon took a large slice of his tract for the bed of the " Lawrence Basin " of the Chestnut Hill Reservoir, and thus deprived it of its bucolic aspect. However, for twenty years this place was his autumn home, and to it he rode almost every day in the year, superintending the plowing, sowing, and reaping, planting nurseries of fruit-trees, pruning and grafting, overseeing the dairy, and giving play to his taste for farming and country life which his ancestry from Wisset, England to Groton had cultivated from necessity.

In 1864 Mr. Lawrence moved for the first time to his summer home at Nahant. With each of the succeeding twenty-two years he became more and more attached to the spot which nature and neighbors made so congenial. The cottage, which

stands on one of the southwest points,
caught the breezes fresh from the water;
the clear sweep of view across Lynn Bay
to the Saugus Hills gave every sunset with
its reflected colors a double glory.; and at
night when Mr. Lawrence lay awake for
hours reflecting and praying, as he often
did, his thoughts were accompanied by the
soft splashing of the waves beneath his window. His love for Boston people intensified as he grew older; and the description
of Nahant society by his near neighbor Mr.
Thomas G. Appleton, "cold roast Boston,"
was to Mr. Lawrence its chief recommenda-
tion. With Mr. Longfellow next door and
with many representatives of Old Boston
all about him, he could cultivate to his
heart's content that social nature which
would not let a day pass without informal
calls on his friends.

Here also it was his pleasure to pass several hours in the saddle, exploring the fields
and rocky points, discovering new views,
chatting with the neighbors in the Irish settlement as well as on the hill, and then taking a sharp canter on the hard sand of Long
Beach. At Nahant the whole family cen-
tred, so that a dinner-table of twelve or fif-

teen children and grandchildren was a familiar scene. These family gatherings were the happiest occasions in his life, so happy as to keep his somewhat morbid temperament in anxiety lest the first gap should soon occur.

Sunday was never complete at Nahant, or at Longwood, without the singing of " psalm tunes " in the evening. Children and guests were all expected to join, and Mr. Lawrence's voice could always be heard leading off in " Dundee," " Federal Street," " Coronation," and other familiar tunes.

This letter to his son suggests his old associations with psalm singing.

Sunday Evening, April 6, 1873.   LONGWOOD.

MY DEAR SON, — We have had half an hour of what I call good music. Some people might dispute this, but they could not doubt about the sentiment. There is no music better than psalm tunes, and no sentiments higher than those contained in the poetry at the end of the Prayer Book, in my opinion. How we used to troll them off at Groton fifty odd years ago. Sunday evening my grandfather would send out for " Oliver " (Wentworth), who lived in the cottage beyond the barn, and who was an humble friend of my grandfather (who took him out of the poor-house when he was a child) and of his descendants for eighty years. Then he would set the tune and Oliver would sing the tenor and my grandmother and Aunt Mary Woodbury and Aunt Eliza and we boys and anybody else who happened to be there would join in. I have never heard any music since that struck my ear like that. I can hear Oliver clearing his throat now for another effort. No doubt the old chap has now a seat somewhere in the heavenly choir. When we abandon the psalms and the Sundays of our forefathers then we shall be carried away captive into Egypt, and we shall never be released except by a miracle. Sometimes it looks as though that is just where we are going, especially hereabouts. We 've set up a great light and we think we can see into all past and future things. But our lantern will be upset some day, and we shall be left in Egyptian darkness, unless we take a back track in time.

Your affectionate father,

A. A. L.

His wife, who was endowed with peculiar beauty and dignity, was the complement of himself, strong where he was weak. If his sentimental or enthusiastic nature was in danger of leading him into unwise action, her sturdy common sense held him in check; if a nervous reaction caused depression of spirits, her even, well-balanced temperament would in time bring him to a healthy view of life. As the greater part of the cares of the large household fell to her, it was fortunate that she had the strength and executive ability to carry them. "If," as he wrote to her father, "Sarah had taken charge of the commissariat of the British army when Miss Nightingale did of the hospitals, the war in the Crimea would have been better conducted than it was."

Mr. Lawrence, however, was not one who could throw all the responsibility of his children's care and development of character upon the mother. Every morning they were called into his dressing-room for private prayer, and in the drives and Sunday walks he had the faculty of interspersing the light conversation with such remarks on people, society, and character as would lead them to a higher sense of duty and the worth of life. Twice every Sunday he accompanied them to church, and, that his example might have its influence upon them as well as others, he worked in the Sunday-school as teacher, superintendent, or librarian. And if prevented from going to church a second time, he sometimes called them to his room and there joined with them in prayer. There was no religious compulsion in the house; the force of example and teaching, joined with a confidence in the children, was alone regarded.

In the education of his sons, he sent them for a time to the public school that they might learn to meet and respect boys of all classes, and he made them learn to use carpenter's tools, and to care for a horse or a garden, that they might appreciate good work in others. He, fortunately for them, had as little regard for high scholastic rank as when he was in college. Next to the development of a good character in young men, he esteemed the habit of a right use of money. He insisted on exact accounts in earliest boyhood, created a realization of the value of money by paying interest on all cash deposited with him, and, when he had tested the ability to save as well as spend, he gave such generous allowances that he could reasonably and successfully ask that savings and gifts to charities should begin in early days. When each of his children became twenty-one, he gave them unreservedly a patrimony which would support them in comfort without any further obligation to himself. He thus made them independent of their parents in fortune, and they were held to the home only by bonds of affection and gratitude.

In fact, so little did the love of accumulation bind Mr. Lawrence that he systematically reduced his property the last thirty years of his life by gifts to his children and charitable or public enterprises.

With the property delivered to each of his children he always sent some such letter as the following to a daughter: " But after all, it is only yours in trust. It will not be long (though it may seem otherwise to you now) before you will be called to give an account of the whole of it. May God help you to use it and all your advantages so as to render an account that will be acceptable to Him. You have been a dutiful and loving daughter, for which I thank God every day of my life."

Or this to his elder son : —

" This property with your profession will give you a good living, and will enable you to lay up something before you have a family of your own, and against 'a rainy day.' But it is not possible for me to enrich my children nor even to give them such a kind of support as some people think is necessary in these extravagant times, nor am I sorry for it. On the contrary, I am glad that my children should have the stimulus to exertion which I myself had. Labor has been to me one of the greatest enjoyments of my life, and one of my greatest blessings, and I hope it may be theirs.

" You cannot expect to be so long and so abundantly blessed as I have been ; but you will be spared from some hardships which fall on those who begin life poor. Property is a trust ; and it affords more or less pleasure in proportion to the fidelity with which we administer it."

In the education of his daughters there was one burden that hung heavily on him through life — the aimless existence which social conventionality gives to the young woman after her school days. In this, as in the strict observance of Sunday and a love of simplicity in dress, he exhibited something of his Puritan ancestry.

He had no patience with those fashionable people who, as he used to say, debauched the young with late hours and excitement. Writing to his daughter he said: " If any of the family went to the party, I hope they set an example of plain dressing and early hours. If anything can be out of place at Nahant, it will be trailing dresses in the scanty space of the cottages and party hours of the city. We dry goods importers and stocking weavers make ourselves and our families ridiculous when we ape the fashions of foreign courts. Don't you agree to that ? If you don't you will when you have seen what the world is made of."

A useful or refining occupation was, in his opinion, one of the necessaries of life. With that feeling he wrote to a niece who was travelling in Europe and who afterwards developed a remarkable taste in embroidery.

My dear ——, — The handsomest present that I have received for a long time was sent to me the other day by a delightful lady now eighty years old, Mrs. Guild, of Brookline, a sister of Mrs. Ticknor. It is the picture of a young robin, rather larger than life, beautifully drawn and painted. It is the best robin I ever saw. Mr. Audubon could not have done it better. What a great pleasure it must be for this ancient lady to be exercising herself in this elegant manner. How much more elevating and refining, than in darning an old pair of stockings, or in taking snuff and tea, and talking about one's neighbors. If you have not yet discovered any particular taste which you can indulge and cultivate, perhaps by looking a little more carefully you will meet with success. And then you will have great pleasure in doing what you find yourself doing so well. You will be pleased to excel others; you will enjoy the admiration of friends and of others. But above all you will be pleased to find yourself doing good, and improving that talent which the good Lord has given you. Good-by my darling.

Your affectionate uncle Lawrence.

That the evil of aimless lives was not to be met by the collegiate education of women, would seem to be his opinion (which was somewhat modified in later years), from a letter in connection with co-education in Kansas

University. " I think there never has been and never will be a high standard of learning in an institution where the sexes are instructed together. Such institutions may be tolerable academies, but never will be first-class colleges. I have no faith in the utility of giving diplomas to women, except for good housewifery, for courage, and for rearing good families of children."

He was not only courteous to his servants, but he had a personal interest in each, and in his conversation with them would vary his anecdotes with friendly advice in such a way as to gain their confidence and affection. They always were welcomed to family prayers, and he would not begin to read the Bible until he was assured that some were present. He followed, with interest, the lives of those who had once served in the house, and for the thirty last years of his life, regularly visited the nurse of his children.

His sense of kinship was very strong. He corresponded with relatives whom he had not seen for a generation. To one of them he writes : " As time wears on and we form new attachments, we think of old friends less often, but the memory of and love for blood relations can never be obliterated. It comes

over one in solitude and sickness with a force
that is not known in the bustle of business
and the rounds of daily life." A family
quarrel was, in his opinion, the most needless
and wicked form of selfishness.

There was one bond of kinship which was
of peculiar strength and tenderness.

With the death of their father, in 1852,
his brother William and he were left the
only representatives of that branch of the
family. The affection which, up to this time,
had bound them together developed into a
closeness of thought, sympathy, and sentiment which steadily strengthened for over
thirty years. His brother, who had been a
traveller of wide experience and some adven-
ture, and who was endowed with a fund of
anecdote and wit, had somewhat remarkable
social traits. He became a physician and
immediately devoted his skill to the poor,
and in their interest was very active in the
organization of the Boston Dispensary. Besides publishing his father's " Diary and
Correspondence," he wrote a book on the
" Charities of France," in the hope of giving
American charities the benefit of the French-
men's experience. Ill health called him to
Europe continually after his marriage; but

while at home he gave strength and time to charities and religious work, especially the organization of Emmanuel Church. His house on Arlington Street was the centre of such forms of activity.

A regular correspondence during William's absence and an almost daily call when living at home, kept the brothers in constant sympathy. A slight illness of one brought the other immediately to his side. Each gave to the other's charitable or patriotic interests. In the development of Longwood they worked and owned together. When therefore, in 1867, Dr. Lawrence built a home next to his brother in Longwood, it seemed to be the last touch to their blessings, and Mr. Lawrence's record of the fact closes with the words, " May God bless our declining years and unite us hereafter; and those whom we have loved with those whom we so much love now."

XIII.

PHILANTHROPIC INTERESTS.

HAVING suggested a few of the more personal traits of Mr. Lawrence in the maturity of his life, we may now return to the record of his interests and activities.

The echo of the last shot of the war had hardly died away before the *alumni* of Harvard College met to arrange for the reception of their brethren who had been in the army. From that there naturally sprang the thought of a memorial, and by August, 1865, Mr. Lawrence had recorded "several meetings of a college committee to erect a Memorial Hall in honor of those of the college who fell in the war." He was made a chairman of the finance committee, which immediately entered upon the task of raising the money. Daily committee meetings, the enthusiasm and untiring industry of Charles G. Loring, J. Ingersoll Bowditch, Stephen M. Weld, Henry B. Rogers, Henry Lee, and other loyal sons of the college, soon brought about happy results.

"Church of Our Saviour"

On February 2, 1866, Mr. Lawrence wrote: "Theodore Lyman came to offer $5,000 for building Memorial Hall at Cambridge, if twenty can be found to do the same."

A letter to one of the older *alumni* tells the story of the earliest subscriptions to the fund, which (with the Sanders bequest and other gifts) finally reached the unexpected amount of $387,000.

BOSTON, *February* 28, 1866.

MY DEAR SIR, — Mr. Richardson of Cambridge, who lost a son in the war, says that he will be one of twenty to give $5,000 each to build the Memorial Hall of the *alumni.* Mr. E. R. Mudge, who lost his oldest son in the same way, offers the same. Theodore Lyman, who served three years and more, offers $5,000. Nathan Appleton, who served three years, does the same.

Now these are not the men to build it. The two first are not *alumni,* and they have already given to their country what is dearer than their own lives ; the other two have offered their lives ; and have endured hardship, and have incurred expense, while most of us *alumni* were living at ease. I have proposed, and it is agreed to by the committee, that the subscribers may pay in instalments, one fifth every year. By this last I am induced to subscribe $5,000. This is hard work and slow. But if we get twenty, then we may be assured of the rest.

My object in writing this is to seize hold of your love for Alma Mater, and to ask you whether, if we get nineteen names, you will be the twentieth subscriber. This would encourage us very much.

Very truly yours,
A. A. L.

The motive of the work is expressed in a letter to his cousin, James Lawrence, from whom he was asking for a subscription. "It seems to be the least that we can do, who did not go to the war, to commemorate the virtues of those who did go, and especially of those who marched and fought and died while we were comfortable at home."

Under the inspiration of this motive, the noble Memorial Hall was erected, and through the energies of Messrs. C. W. Eliot, Lee, and Bowditch, and of Mr. Lawrence, who added efficient financial support, the college was furnished with a far better play-ground than the Delta on which the hall stands.

The next two objects of Mr. Lawrence's activity have to do with his religious and church life.

His journals and letters reveal a simple faith, a deep, personal piety, and a realization of the heavenly life which are as difficult to attain as they are rare among men who, like himself, move in the midst of business, political, and social activities. As long as he lived in Boston, he attended St. Paul's Church, of which he was the treasurer for several years. For some time after his removal to Longwood, his loyalty to St. Paul's and devotion to Dr. Vinton led him to go to Boston to service. But, wishing always to take his family, he found it more convenient to go to St. Paul's Church, Brookline, where, as usual, he did work as vestryman and in the Sunday-school. The sympathetic nature of Mr. Lawrence was never content with official pastoral association. Between himself and his minister there always existed such friendly and personal relations as made him almost as necessary to them as they were to him. These few lines from his journal suggest the tenderness of the relations : —

" October 7, 1853. Friday morning at six was sent for by Rev. Dr. Stone; hastened to his house; went up-stairs and into his chamber; found him sitting up in bed partially paralyzed. I put my arm around him and endeavored to encourage him; and he soon appeared to rally his spirits. I asked him if he wished to send for any of his friends, Mr. Upham, Mr. Aspinwall, or others. He answered, ' No, Amos, you are friend enough for me,' throwing his arms about my neck."

In fact the same regard for ministers of high character and varied creeds which made his father the friend of President Mark Hopkins, Dr. Palfrey, Dr. Lothrop, Father Taylor, Father Mathew, and others, seemed to descend to the son.

His house was always open to the clergymen of the younger as well as the older generation, but, with few exceptions, his friendship was confined to the latter. Bishop Eastburn was for years his next-door neighbor, and into his house Mr. Lawrence carried the dying form of Bishop Griswold, who had fallen at the steps. Drs. Vinton, Stone, Lothrop, Wharton, Peabody, and Professor Packard were all close to him in friendly or intimate sympathy. Dr. Mark Hopkins made an annual visit. Dr. Henry C. Potter was his nearest neighbor as long as he was assistant minister of Trinity Church. Of him Mr. Lawrence at that time wrote : " He is a finished writer and preacher, and fine-looking. If he has his health, he will be a noted divine of our church and a bishop." To Cottage Farm, Bishop Paddock first came after his election; and he was one of the last guests before the death of Mr. Lawrence at Nahant.

Two old saints he kept near him to give, as it were, a benediction to his office and to his home. On account of his kindly relations with the venerable city missionary, Dr. E. M. P. Wells, Mr. Lawrence became the guardian of the small fund provided for his personal needs; for, like the saints of old, the doctor gave away everything. He was therefore a frequent visitor at the office, and many an hour was snatched from business to listen to his holy conversation. " If Father Wells does not get to heaven, then none of us can expect to reach that much-expected home. He is eighty years old, I believe. He lost everything by the fire ; but he says he gained more than he lost, *i. e.*, grace :

the other could not help him long." In Longwood, the oldest presbyter in the diocese lived and died in a house provided by Mr. Lawrence, who took even more satisfaction in presence of his neighbor than did the grateful clergyman in the comfort of his home.

The same hatred of wasted spiritual energies which moved him as a young man at Bedford, where many churches were built for the few inhabitants, followed him through life. It was from this point of view that he criticised and avoided sectarianism. It was more than unchristian; it was unbusinesslike. In 1870, finding his name attached to an appeal for an organization which he felt would provoke partisanship, he wrote : —

My dear Sir, — The Church consists of all those who love the Lord Jesus Christ and obey his precepts. And of all the denominations into which, through human weakness and ignorance, it has become divided, I believe the Protestant Episcopal Church is the best. On that account I joined it nearly forty years ago, and my love for it has increased ever since. But this does not prevent my loving Christians of other denomi-

nations and acting with them ; and especially
it does not prevent my living and acting
with those of my own denomination who entertain opinions in which there are " shades
of difference." No doubt this movement to
make all men of one mind will gain adher-
ents, and churchmen may become so hostile
to each other as to divide the Church many
times ; but all this will not make men agree,
nor will it advance the truth nor the cause
of religion.

Holding these views, my name is out of
place in your organization.

With sentiments of esteem for yourself
and for the other gentlemen of the board,

I remain your obedient servant,

A. A. L.

It was in this spirit that, when he found
the Methodists established in Wisconsin, he
placed the funds of Lawrence University in
their hands. When he went to a village or
summer resort where there was but one
church, he always worshipped in that. When
prevented by storm from attending his own
church at Lynn, he was to be seen in the
Methodist meeting-house listening to the
local preacher, or a negro exhorter. For

some months he was a teacher in the church founded by Mr. Sears, the " Searsarian Church," as Mr. Lawrence used to call it. He would never allow himself to be classified with a party, and was one of the first vice - presidents of the Church Congress, which he felt would lead to mutual understanding and forbearance.

It was also a satisfaction to him that, at the General Convention of 1865, to which he was a delegate, there occurred the reconciliation of the church, which had been divided by the war.

When party feeling was running high, he wrote to his daughter, who, while at school in New York, attended St. George's Church, of which Dr. Tyng was rector: —

"October 12, 1869. Rev. Dr. Tyng has written a remarkable letter. He is a zealous man. But he is a revolutionist. He is in favor of making a new Prayer Book, and of throwing away the old one. This, he thinks, will make a new church. I guess it will. But it will not be a large one. It will rather be an offshoot of a gnarly growth from the parent church, and what used to be called a schism, and that is the right name for it. The doctor is a good Tyng; but he

is a ' Tyng ' nevertheless. If you were a
hundred years old, you would know what
that means. I don't believe in making di-
visions in the Church, but in healing them.
Protestantism is sometimes called a failure
because it has led to the formation of many
sects. We should have charity for each
other, and agree to differ about minor
things."

The church at Nahant was a source of great
satisfaction to him. The preachers, Sunday
after Sunday, are of different denominations,
and the worshippers conform to the manner
of worship of the denomination represented
by the preacher. For many years two dea-
cons were chosen to invite and entertain the
ministers. Mr. Lawrence always took his
turn as deacon, and looked forward with
pleasure to the entertainment of the clergymen. He always spoke with great satisfaction of the fact that for over fifty years
people of different creeds had worshipped
together without a jar, and he gave his support to the church as an outpost of Christian
unity. In memory of his interest and bene-
factions the proprietors have placed a tablet
in the wall of the church.

By 1867 Longwood had developed into

quite a community. With a sense of responsibility for the spritual welfare of the people
whom they had drawn together, Mr. Lawrence and his brother joined in building a
stone church in memory of their father. In
March, 1868, it was consecrated under the
name of "The Church of our Saviour," and
was presented to a corporation, to be held
in trust. With a wish to interest the people
in the work, Mr. Lawrence and his brother
persistently refused to be conspicuous in the
church, and, when possible, sat far back, that
there might be no thought on the part of
others of proprietorship. For years a good
part of the financial burden fell upon them ;
but, while always taking it, their object was
to educate the people into a sense of responsibility in the support of public worship.

As early as 1852 Mr. Lawrence had urged
the building of galleries in St. Paul's Church,
Boston, that seats might be made for poor
persons. Therefore, with a desire to do
everything to make the building a church
for all the people, the brothers entered with
enthusiasm some years later into making all
the seats free. During the last year of his
life, while Mrs. Lawrence was giving a stone
rectory, he presented some property to be

held in trust for the preservation and support of the church.

It was a sight seen oftener in old England than in this country, — the two venerable brothers with their families joining the group of neighbors, as they walked to the door of the memorial church, then worshipping together like one large family. On week-days as well as Sundays, they might both be found with the little company of faithful worshippers. As if to continue their close association there, a memorial tablet records their names, with the inscription : —

TOGETHER THEY BUILT THIS CHURCH IN MEMORY OF THEIR FATHER, AMOS LAWRENCE.

LOVELY AND PLEASANT IN THEIR LIVES, AND IN THEIR DEATH THEY WERE NOT DIVIDED.

Early in 1867 Mr. Benjamin T. Reed gave $100,000 towards the foundation of an Episcopal Theological School, and, having the intention of finally devoting his whole fortune to the object, he called about him a board of five trustees, composed of Robert C. Winthrop, James S. Amory, Edward S. Rand, J. P. Putnam, and Mr. Lawrence.

The munificence of the gift and its religious object appealed to the interest of Mr.

Lawrence. Moreover, in the plan he saw a long-desired opportunity to bring a more positive religious element into the neighborhood of Harvard College. The religious influences at Cambridge had been a source of anxiety to him, and he had always felt that the identification of a Unitarian Divinity School with the college was a positive injury to both, and as a member of the corporation he had urged some change. When, therefore, the question of a site for the Theological School was raised, and when some of Mr. Reed's friends advised strongly against Cambridge on account of its Unitarian and negative religious influence, Mr. Lawrence joined with others in pressing the establishment of the site in Cambridge, and as near the college as possible. They felt convinced (and experience has justified their conviction) that the contact with the university life would be an advantage to the school, and that the school and its chapel might exert a positive influence upon the life of the university. As usual, the position of treasurer, which he continued to hold for fifteen years, fell to his lot, and he again took up his rides through the Cambridge roads which had been so familiar to him when treasurer of the college. His satisfaction in the work was enhanced by the renewed association with two of his old pastors, Drs. Stone and Wharton, who were called to fill chairs in the new institution. His familiarity with the place made him active in the selection of sites, and in 1869 the school laid its permanent foundations in its present beautiful position, the choice of which was hastened by the offer by his old partner, Robert M. Mason, to build St. John's Memorial Chapel.

Mr. Lawrence determined to mark his gratitude for thirty years of exceptional blessings in the way expressed in this letter to the trustees of the school : —

(Near) BOSTON, *June* 23, 1873.

GENTLEMEN, — More than a year ago, on the anniversary of my marriage, I was so much impressed with the remembrance of the great goodness of God to myself and my numerous family, during the thirty years which have elapsed without any cessation to our prosperity and happiness, that I wished to make some acknowledgment, and to have some permanent, and if possible some useful memorial of it.

Therefore, after purchasing the requisite amount of land, I commenced the building of a dormitory for the use of our theological students, corresponding with the chapel and with the plan of building adopted by the trustees. Before the next meeting this work will be done so far as to accommodate twenty students, and the rooms will be furnished. At a future time, if it should be required, I may complete the design by adding twenty rooms more.

Meantime, having placed a brief inscription over the entrance, to indicate the circumstances which conduced to its erection, I beg to present the whole to the trustees, in the hope that it will be useful in advancing the cause for which we are associated, and which we all have at heart.

Faithfully yours,   A. A. L.

In 1873 the first half of the building was completed, and in 1880 the second half was added, making one side of the open quadrangle, which, with the chapel and other buildings since presented by Mr. Reed and Mr. John A. Burnham, now form a picturesque group of stone.

Over the door of the dormitory stands this inscription : —

"Lawrence hall"

IN · MEMORIAM · SUMMÆ ·
DEI · BENEVOLENTIÆ
PRID · KAL · APRIL · M D CCC LXXII ·

During the term of his treasurership, Mr. Lawrence had the usual privilege of advancing money and helping to make up deficits, but he had the satisfaction of seeing the school develop in strength far beyond the expectation of its founder.

XIV.

MATURE YEARS.

1867–1882.

In 1867 the active routine of twenty-five years had begun to affect Mr. Lawrence's health ; he had the first sharp warnings of indigestion, neuralgia, and depression of spirits, and by the doctor's advice decided to pass a summer in Europe. His social disposition never allowed him to travel alone ; the larger the party the more he enjoyed a journey. If at any time a trip to the South or West was advised by the physician (and a physician's advice alone could drive him from home), he called on some friends to make up a company. His cousin, Dr. Samuel A. Green, was always ready to start with him, or with any of his family, at twenty-four hours' notice. On this summer journey, in which he renewed the memories of his bachelor travels, he had a family party of twelve, which partially compensated him for the loss of home life; though even under these circumstances he felt restless and sometimes homesick until he recrossed the Channel and was driving through the homelike fields and lanes of England. The break of routine enabled him to return refreshed to added responsibilities.

The business of the Cocheco and Salmon Falls Companies had increased very much on Mr. Lawrence's hands, but experience and system had put them into such shape that he was able to enlarge his work. Feeling that this country ought not to be dependent upon others for the clothing of her people, and believing that the skill and industry of the New Englander would, if temporarily protected, produce cheaper and better goods than Old England could supply, he was tempted to become a manufacturer as well as a commission merchant and a farmer.

Therefore in 1860 he bought a mill at Ipswich for the manufacture of hosiery and other knit goods. But the industry was a new one in this country, the machinery was crude, the labor unskilled, and the American people had not realized that hosiery could be made here, and therefore refused to buy anything with an American mark. The experiment resulted at first in heavy and steady losses. For years Ipswich was a receptacle for profits from other sources. In January, 1868, Mr. Lawrence wrote: "Am starting up my mill at Ipswich again, which has been stopped for a few weeks. This attempt to manufacture cotton stockings by machinery so that they can be sold at $1.50 a dozen has caused me to lose not less than $100 a day for 800 days, $80,000. Yet I am not discouraged, though I feel the loss very much, for I want a great deal of money to use." If at any time for several years he was attacked with indigestion, it was his habit to lay it, with good reason, to "too much Ipswich."

However, after a hard and persistent struggle of twenty years, he had the satisfaction of seeing his object gained, cheap American stockings and other knit goods sold by the million to the American people. And it was with the greatest pleasure that he saw his friends and family buying goods of his own manufacture under the impression given by the salesmen at the retail shop that they were French or English. This interest, which was increased later by the purchase of the Gilmanton and Ashland Mills in New Hampshire, made him the largest knit goods manufacturer in the country and led him to encourage the formation of the Association of Knit Goods Manufacturers, of which he was president for some time, as he had been of the National Association of Cotton Manufacturers and Planters.

In 1870 he also took the selling agency of the Arlington Mills in Lawrence, which increased rapidly and added to his responsibility.

The manufacture of knit goods brought him into closer relations than ever with the tariff question, and caused his recommendations to have great weight in the construction of the earlier knit goods tariff bills. Few things are more dreary than the rehearsal of tariff discussions; it may be enough, therefore, to say that Mr. Lawrence, in the earlier part of his business life, advocated a high tariff for the protection of infant industries, but as years passed he believed in the gradual reduction of that protection, and in later years he was very positive in the advocacy of more moderate duties, especially on raw materials.

In all his business relations Mr. Lawrence was quick to decide and to act; besides judgment, he had that other trait necessary to success in business — courage ; he readily caught the point of a problem, and was restless until it was answered. He would chafe at listening to an explanation which was a few minutes too long, and then would turn to sit patiently for a half an hour while some missionary from the West or an agent of a charitable society would slowly unfold his tale. Experience led him to believe more and more in system, and to shrink from attending to details himself.

Writing to his elder son, who had just entered business with him, he said, " Losses are made in a day, while profits are a long time accumulating. Let us adopt a good system and then not be anxious about results." " It is not easy to save money in commission and manufacturing business, and much skill and judgment are required in both. The cause is this, that it is difficult to avoid losses, much more difficult than it is to make profits. I am led to make this remark from looking over L. & Co.'s trial balance."

The faculty of quick decision and systematizing enabled Mr. Lawrence to bring the hours of his own business into a very short compass. The greater part of office hours was given to other people's affairs. Besides the public interests already described, he was active in establishing a line of steamships from Boston to New Orleans and was president of the company; he was also the first president of the New England Trust Company, and a director in the Massachusetts Hospital Life Company and in a number of manufacturing and mercantile corporations. As an officer of the Massachusetts Society of the Cincinnati, the Bunker Hill Monument Association, the Massachusetts Society for Promoting Agriculture, and the Home for Aged Men, he took a lively interest in these associations. When Dr. Howe, with his inextinguishable love of liberty, espoused the cause of the Cretans in their struggle with the Turks, his Kansas memories prompted him to turn to Mr. Lawrence to act as treasurer of the funds. All such duties, as well as the giving to deserving objects, were accompanied with a sense of satisfaction; but there was one class whom, on account of his sympathetic nature, he unconsciously encouraged, and yet whom he could not treat with patience, — the chronic borrowers. The only satisfaction he ever took in lending to such people was the hope, which was usually a 'forlorn one, that they would not show their faces again. The following is one of a mass of letters which tell the same story : —

BOSTON, *August* 9, 1872.

DEAR SIR, — A large sheet might be covered with the reasons why I cannot lend money, not even to my nearest friends. But I will only say that it would be as safe as taking out the bung from a barrel of cider. In my case it is the only barrel in the house. It is good cider and the bung is in the bottom, as the barrel lays.

For twenty years I have been busy writing letters, with reasons. For ten years before that I lent some money, and wrote some letters. In both cases I was the loser, and don't think anybody was the gainer.

Yours truly,　　　　A. A. L.

His resolution not to lend was better than his practice, for on several occasions his sympathy for acquaintances in financial distress lead him into heavy losses. But that no ill will was harbored is seen by this letter to a person who had borrowed several thousand dollars, who announced a few days after that he had failed.

Boston, *November* 13, 1873.

My dear Sir, — Your note is received with great regret, chiefly on your account (I trust) and not on mine ; for your disappointment must be infinitely greater than mine can be. You have been most unfortunate ; but nobody has said that you have been in fault, that I ever heard, except in judgment. And many great and good men have erred strangely in their judgment of business matters. Rev. Mr. Beecher says he rather thinks that those who are most unfortunate in this world (without intentionally doing wrong) will be the favored ones in the next, and he says that if he takes off his hat in the street to any man, it will be to him who has struggled to do his duty and who has in a good measure succeeded in that ; but who has failed in achieving any worldly success.

I am rather of Mr. Beecher's opinion.

Yours truly,   A. A. L.

In one form of beneficence he took keen delight ; that of sending unexpected gifts to literary men whose salaries were such as to demand strict economy. Now and again a box of fine tea or a check or a cloak would be delivered at the door of some professor at Bowdoin, Williams, or Harvard, accompanied by a brief line which gave grace to the gift. He could not open a fresh box of cigars without the satisfaction of feeling that some clergyman had a duplicate. The old librarian of Harvard College, whose economy was only exceeded by his generosity, pours out his thanks for a new cloak; "Mrs. S. has been chiding me a long time for wearing my old one till it has now got to be the twenty-ninth winter, and says she is delighted; and she desires me to express her gratitude for your practical wisdom in trying 'to make me look decent.'"

At sixty years of age Mr. Lawrence was still active in body and bright in society, but his nervous system was weakened. Neuralgia again laid its torturing grasp on him and depression of spirits resulted. To those who suffered like him he gave good advice. To a farmer in Maine he wrote: "You write as though your spirits were poor. But you must remember that this is the season when the bile is stagnant. Take a little good cider with your dinner; take a little in the morning before breakfast with saleratus in it. Put a strengthening plaster on your back between your shoulders. Take a little whiskey if it suits. Go out and sit on the warm side of the house, and listen to the birds in the morning."

To his friend Le Baron, who suffered from the same trouble, he sent word, " Now, my dear old Baron, I charge nothing for my advice. Brom. potas. is good: so is quinine ; and bismuth ; and some whiskey. But God holds the key of our minds."

Still he found it hard to act always on his own advice.

In trying to help friends in business he had met with some losses which were more annoying than serious; the fall of his horse upon his ankle had cut off his customary exercise — and, more than all, four children had married and had left his house for homes of their own. " What strikes me most is the quickness with which our children have come and gone," he wrote to his son ; and one great dread of his life was the thought, " What shall we do if we live till all our children have left us ? " He took great satisfaction in the way that each of them left home, and yet he never could reconcile himself to their absence. The house had been so full of noise and activity for years, and he had become accustomed to the echo of young voices in the halls, that even the absence of some of the family for a short visit would depress him. His sympathetic nature was not satisfied without the presence of those whom he loved, but the very intensity of his sympathy made him a poor nurse and assistant in the sick room. At about this time sickness took its first strong hold in the family. In 1870 Mrs. Lawrence, who had borne the cares of the large household, suffered in health for some months, but was restored by a few weeks with Mr. Lawrence and a part of the family in Europe. In 1875 a son who was just entering work in the ministry was stricken with typhoid fever; at the same time a daughter was brought to the point of death. In the long illness of the latter, lasting two or three years, Mr. Lawrence followed the even course of his life, though consumed by anxiety; and the only outlet for his sympathies was found in visiting the sick in other houses. He had always been a frequent visitor when friends were ill or in trouble, but from this time the habit became constant. The object in his ride was almost always an invalid. Such an afternoon as this was his frequent routine.

" February 2. Went in a sleigh with Sarah to visit Tom Knowles (my farmer's son), who is failing by consumption. Then to see Harry Slade, of the same age, who has the same disease. Poor boys! So early laid on the bed of suffering and death. May God in his mercy comfort them, and prepare them for his heavenly kingdom. Visited old sick neighbor, Mr. Hichborn."

Then came a shock from an unexpected quarter as told in his journal.

" Nahant, July 1, 1879. Dr. Williams told me that a 'cataract' is forming in my right eye. It made itself known by a blurred, cloudy appearance before the spyglass through which I was looking to the sea from my piazza. God give me grace and strength to bear this and all the ills of this body with fortitude, and, if possible, with cheerfulness, knowing that He will never afflict except in mercy."

However, he held to the routine of his life, but the proportion of time given to the different pursuits changed. His son Amory was now able to relieve him of a large part of the responsibility of the business, though Mr. Lawrence went daily to the office for two or three hours and gave his advice in the more important matters. He also held to his other interests, and even entered upon new ones. Tom Hughes' Rugby experiment appealed to his love of enterprise and faith in good settlements. Elected an overseer of Harvard University, he took a keen interest in all the discussions, which at that time were exceptional in brilliancy and ability on account of the important reforms then in view. And his short, quaint speeches added strength and humor to the debates. To the last he opposed the spirit of secularization of the college.

Hearing of the struggle of the Misses Smith of Glastonbury, who allowed their property to be sold for taxes because they as women had no voice in the appropriation of the taxes, he went to their rescue with letters and money, and with some chivalry expressed his views.

" The taxation of the property of women without allowing them any representation in town affairs is so unjust that it seems only necessary to bring it to public notice to excite the interest of all honest voters to make a change. Therefore you deserve the greater honor for resisting that injustice, and for seting an example which must lead to reform.

"Your case has its parallel in every township in New England. In the town where this is written a widow pays $7,830, while six hundred men, a number equal to half the whole number of voters, pay $1,200 in all. Another lady pays $5,042. Yet neither has a single vote, not even by proxy. That is, each one of six hundred men who have no property and pay only a poll tax, many of whom cannot read or write, has the power of voting away the property of the town, while the females have no power at all.

"We have lately spent a day in celebrating the heroism of those who threw over the tea; but how trifling was the tea tax and how small the injustice to individuals compared with this one of our day. The principle, however, is the same, that there should be no taxation without representation."

To a gentleman who hoped that another woman suffragist had been raised up, he stated his opinions in a more positive way.

BOSTON, *October* 14, 1874.

DEAR SIR, — Universal (manhood) suffrage has proved to be a failure in the cities and thickly settled communities, and all through the South: chiefly because it is not based on intelligence, nor on character, nor on property. To give the right to vote to all the women would only be to increase the evil.

It seems to me that the women who are taxed should have the right to vote, and if that is refused, they have the right to rebel: and the men would have a right to help them, that is, those who chose to.

Yours truly,   A. A. L.

With the approach of old age he naturally turned with pleasure to the scenes of his boyhood. As his younger son was rector of Grace Church, Lawrence, Mr. Lawrence was enabled to visit the North Parish, Andover, and look up the old school-house, which he recognized transformed into a barn; he took intense delight in talking over the days with his former school-mates Surgeon General Dale and Captain Chever; and as long as the poor old sexton John Frye lived in his filthy hovel, Mr. Lawrence insisted on sending money to keep him out of the poor-house, where the town authorities insisted that he ought to go.

His associations with Groton had been kept up by correspondence and occasional visits. He was still interested in the affairs

and people of the town, as the following letter to his aunt Eliza (Mrs. Green), who had
cared for him after the death of his mother,
and with whom he kept up an affectionate
correspondence for over fifty years, shows.

BOSTON, *March* 29, 1871.

MY DEAR AUNT, — If you ever see Mr.
Spaulding who makes the cider, will you be
good enough to give my compliments to him
and inform him that there is one denomination of Christians who will not think worse
of him for having made such a delightful
and wholesome drink. I do not believe that
his success in this particular would of itself
entitle him to be received and duly enrolled
as a member of the Protestant Episcopal
Church; but it would be counted in among
his other virtues, of which he is said to have
many. With this I send a pamphlet which
will explain the theory and practice of that
religious denomination, which you perhaps
will hand to him. Though it says nothing
about making cider or drinking it, it will be
easily inferred from it that he who makes
good cider, and gives good measure, for a
reasonable price, is so far a public benefac-
tor. And that is true of Mr. Spaulding.

There is a story that he has been excluded from the Groton church for the exercise of this homely art of making good cider, and on that account I have written this letter. With love to all,

Your affectionate nephew,

A. A. L.

But with the death of his aunts and friends in Groton, his memories became so tender and sad that he did not dare to go there often.

The death of old black Peter Hazard, who had been a pensioner of the family for three generations, called him back once, and the simple country funeral is thus described : —

" November 12, 1880. Went to Groton with Dr. Green to bury my old friend, Peter Hazard, who was one hundred and one years old. It was a primitive country funeral at Peter's house (mine, which he has lived in free of rent) by the Nashua river, on the borders of my woods : not another house in sight. There were his two married daughters and their children, and many friends, white and colored. A good service of singing, prayer, and exhortation by Mr. Robie, the Orthodox minister. Then we shook hands with the relatives and drove away. Peter's body lay in a handsome coffin, dressed in his best clothes, and looking as though he were asleep. Good old Peter, farewell, we hope not forever. It is sixty and more years since our acquaintance began. Then you swam with me on your shoulders across the Nashua, and held me on your knee, and cared for me when I was weak and recovering from a fever. My grandfather and grandmother and all of us loved Peter and his sister Lucy, peaceful, kind members of our Groton family. Sam Green took me to the burial ground where rest the bodies of our relatives and friends. I read their dear names on the headstones: I looked off to the grand old Wachusett and Monadnock, the mountains which bounded my boyish world. They brought back the old memories of my childhood. How brief seemed this life! how worthless much that men prize! I hardly knew whether I was living in the present or the past. God help us all to live as in thy presence, and without sin, ready to go hence at thy summons, to meet those who have been dear to us, and whom we believe to be with Thee in heaven.

" Went over the old homestead, which

James has enlarged and beautified. Here came the memories again. Sam was sad, and so was I ; but we talked of old times and laughed away our tears. Reached home after dark."

On the last Christmas of his life he gave his cousin, Dr. Samuel A. Green (who was his ready agent in many charities and in the purchase of a rich collection of Revolutionary and Rebellion literature for the Massachusetts Historical Society), $400 for distribution among sixteen old persons in Groton.

Two occupations steadily increased, — his out-of-door life and his visits on the sick and aged. Though his eyesight was failing, he either continued in the saddle, or else he would take some young neighbor or other companion to drive. Except when the neuralgia caught him, no weather was too rough, and until he was seventy he knew no greater delight than a good skate on Jamaica Pond or a coast down Amory's Hill.

Every morning Mr. Lawrence would start in his buggy for the counting-room, but it was seldom that he reached there without calling at some houses on the way, to inquire for some sick one, to leave a few pats of fresh butter for an invalid, or to take a pink to his grandson, Amos. A few lines from his journal tell the story and suggest the variety of his friends.

"November 30. Sick calls. To Alanson Tucker, who is in bed, and sees no one but his family. Visited Mrs. James K. Mills. She looks worn and ill. But she was glad to converse, and grateful for kindness.

"December 1. Visited my old friend, Mrs. Clapp, at the Brunswick hotel. She is a widow, and lives alone. Called on sick Mrs. Ryan in the village ; gave her money. Then on old Mr. Warren and his wife. Took them clothes, very poor. Then Miss Laura Rogers, who mourns the loss of her aunt, my old friend, Martha C. Derby.

" 2. Visited my friend, Henry B. Rogers, who has been in Europe since the death of his wife. He and his daughter Annette live together. Seemed glad to see me. Excellent people.

"Visited the widow of the late Rev. Dr. Andrew Bigelow. She was delighted to see me. She is a Spiritualist, and immediately gave me a communication from my mother ; also from my uncle Abbott. She talked fluently and well. Gave her twenty dollars for her poor."

But the spring of 1882 opened sadly for Mr. Lawrence. Though he fully realized his exceptionally happy surroundings, yet ill attuned nerves and neuralgia had depressed his spirits; only one child was left in the home where seven had once lived; death had been busy among his old friends; his failing sight had caused him an injury by falling, and had made him less confident in walking.

"My eyesight grows feebler with cataract," he wrote; "one is almost gone. With age must come the loss of our faculties, one by one. If it leads us to look upwards more, for heavenly light, then the loss may be changed to gain."

In May, however, occurred the great sorrow of his life, — the death of his oldest daughter, Mary. Up to this time, the unity of Mr. Lawrence's family had been remarkable. On the preceding Thanksgiving Day he had been able to record: "In the afternoon assembled all our children and grandchildren; all who have been born to us. How remarkable, after nearly forty years of married life, to have health and life continued — twenty-five in all." The married children lived in Longwood or Boston, with the exception of one son who was only an hour away in Lawrence. But Mary, who with her husband, Dr. Amory, and her child lived near by, was in and out of the house continually. Her handsome, bright face and cheery laugh were likely to break in upon the quiet homestead at any moment. In her girlhood, Mr. Lawrence had written of her with perfect truth: " She is truthful, conscientious, kind to all, and I trust sincerely religious. Everything she does affords me pleasure, because she does it cheerfully and as though it were her duty. Her religion seems to be of a practical and at the same time of a cheerful kind."

And yet though he was so easily depressed by the slight illness of a child, or by his own indisposition, he was one of those who seem to take the heavy blows with perfect equanimity.

From the first hour of her short illness until months after her death, a stranger would never have guessed the anguish in his heart. He was as calm as she in the face of death, and with composure prayed with her as she was dying. After all was over, he was more than ever tender and gracious in meeting every one; as was his habit he continued to whistle unconsciously as he worked and walked, and on the day of the funeral began again his routine of calls. After the services in the church in which she had worked and for which she had devoted some of her best energies, her body was laid to rest in Forest Hills. But Mr. Lawrence seemed to take the spirit of her life with him, as he wrote on his return: "Dear Mary: dear, good, lovely, and loving daughter, may you rest in the dear Saviour's arms, and may we follow the example of your good life, until we too are called to meet you in heaven. God grant this for Jesus' sake."

Longwood. Dec. 31st. 1873.
11 P.M.

My dear Son

It is just twenty years at this very hour since my dear Father left us for his Heavenly home. It seems to have been a brief period of time to those of us who are old; and yet it has carried us from vigorous manhood to the verge of old age: and you who are younger from childhood to manhood. Twenty years more will have carried us of the older generation beyond the verge

of time into the life eternal.
May God in His infinite mercy
give us grace and strength to
live according to His Will so as
finally to meet His approval:
and so that we may be ready
and willing to give up our
final account. I know how
far short we come from
the perfect performance of duty: but I hope and confide
in His Mercy for the pardon
of our negligence and of our
sins honestly confessed and
repented of: thro. Jesus Christ
our Lord.   Your affect. father
                    Amos A Lawrence

XV.

1882–1886.

IT will be remembered that Mr. Lawrence had entered business for himself, and by his own ability had reached his present position. In the mean time the old firm of A. & A. Lawrence & Co. had dissolved and their large business had been distributed among different firms. The largest selling agency, that of the Pacific Mills, had been given to Messrs. James L. Little & Co., who in 1882 resigned the charge. It was with great satisfaction that Mr. Lawrence learned that the directors of the Pacific Mills had offered the agency to his firm of Lawrence & Co., for it was the indorsement by those best able to judge of his own business capacity and success, and it was a fitting climax to his mercantile life. Moreover, a return of this great agency to the family was significant of their ability to handle it.

His record is characteristic.

"January 6, 1883. The Pacific Mills Corporation, through its directors (all of whom signed the proposition), have offered to my firm the direction of their vast business, the largest in the United States. May God direct us to a right decision; and if we undertake it, may He give us success and wisdom to use the results in his service, and not in selfish gratification; so that we, and our children after us, may not be damaged by it. Amen."

It required courage to assume, at his age, new and heavy responsibilities, and to reorganize the firm by calling in new partners; but with the help of his son he undertook it, throwing off the smaller selling agencies and retaining only the Cocheco and Salmon Falls with the Pacific. .

Other new philanthropic interests gave him thought and work. At this time he realized more than ever the evils of the liquor traffic, and its baneful effects in politics and social life; and he threw himself with much activity into several forms of temperance work, especially the Law and Order League.

Utah was also drawing the attention of

the people through the efforts of Congress to suppress Mormonism. Here seemed to be another opportunity, by self - sacrificing immigration, to fill Utah with Christian citizens and to free the Territory from the curse, as Kansas was freed from slavery a generation ago. Mr. Eli Thayer, Mr. Branscomb (one of the first Kansas agents), the Rev. Edward Everett Hale, Mr. Williams, and other Kansas veterans, now joined forces again, organized, obtained a charter, and at the expense of Mr. Lawrence sent out scouts to Utah to study the country and the opportunities for an emigrant crusade. It was touching to see these men, now old if not infirm, calling others together in Mr. Lawrence's parlor to polish again their rusty instruments of patriotic emigration for this campaign. But it was of no use. The immediate reason for dropping the scheme was the discovery that the Mormons had possession of all the available farming land; but in fact a new generation had risen, the moral enthusiasm and the crisis were wanting, and the leaders were men who could never again rouse the energies of the rising life as they had in Kansas days. The work, however, gave Mr. Lawrence many busy and happy hours.

In September, 1883, the last wedding took place from Longwood. Mr. Lawrence wrote on the day of the wedding : " Our last unmarried child has left us. All have homes of their own. God be praised for his goodness to us ! Henceforth, ' forgetting those things which are behind, let us reach forth unto those things which are before, and press toward the mark of the prize of the high calling of God in Christ Jesus.' Dear wife ! dear children ! how my heart goes out to you all ! Let us rejoice evermore."

"September 30. My dear wife Sarah and I are now living in our house alone, as when we were first married. Dear, good wife she has been to me, the light of my life and my chief worldly support. May we live together hereafter forever ! But our house does seem lonely with all our children gone out of it. God alone can support and cheer us now, near life's end. To Him I look for light to illumine the darkness which deepens as years increase."

He tried to drive away the sense of loneliness with renewed calls. He became a Visitor of the Associated Charities in Roxbury, and went about among the sick neighbors. Many afternoons were passed like this:

" Very cold wind. Walked to Brookline ; called on Moses Kimball (74), hurt on railroad, very bright and cheerful. Called on old Madame Wakefield (90). She embraced me. Deaf and failing, but still strong ; poor old woman. To Brother William's as usual. Dined at six o'clock."

But his mental depression and sensitive nerves reacted on each other. He writes: " December 20. Neuralgia. Pain, pain ; sinking of the heart for many days and nights. Father in heaven, put under me thy everlasting arms, and sustain me and comfort me."

Thinking that the society of friends and children in Boston would cheer him, he and Mrs. Lawrence lived for three or four months in the house of their daughter, who was in Europe for her health, and here, with his friends, James S. Amory Robert C. Winthrop, William R. Robeson, Dr. Hodges, and others, as near neighbors, and with children and relatives frequently calling, he passed the time happily.

He was now able to renew his attendance at the Thursday Evening Club, and the Massachusetts Historical Society, of which he had been a member for many years.

For thirty years it had been his unfulfilled expectation to visit Kansas, to see the places and the people so familiar by name, and the university which his bounty had founded. After declining many urgent invitations from Governor Robinson and the hospitable citizens, he at last, in 1884, made the journey. He looked for a quiet visit, such as his health would endure, but the reception was so generous and overwhelming that it was too much for his sympathies, and, for fear lest he should break down altogether, he beat a hasty retreat from the grateful people.

The spring of 1884 had brought its harvest of deaths of the aged, among them his business associate of forty-one years, Mr. Mather, whose regularity at the office had hardly suggested to others the thought of age. Mr. James S. Amory had also dropped from the ranks of his dearest friends.

During the summer, Mr. Lawrence still rode his mare " Pet " along the rocky shores of Nahant, though his eyesight was failing ; and, as he wrote on his seventy-first birthday, " Sarah, my dear, devoted wife, remains to be my companion and helper, the guardian angel of my house and of my heart. Though she and I are left alone in our house, it is because our children have made happy homes of their own, and the eldest, our dear Mary, has, we trust, a happier home in the heavens."

Another year of the same routine, short business hours, long drives, short rides, many calls and letters of sympathy to others, passed away. He retired from some duties, such as the position on the Board of Trustees of the Episcopal Theological School, and the Overseers of Harvard College. He met the old Class of '35 for the last time at Commencement, as he writes : —

"June 25. *Fiftieth Anniversary* of our graduation at Cambridge. Twenty-one survivors of our class met in Holworthy. Some had not met for fifty years. Dear old boys! How cheery they were! Boys over again. I thank God for having spared my life so long. More than half of our whole number (fifty-eight) have gone on before. To-day there were present E. Appleton, C. V. Bemis, H. G. O. Blake, John Carr of Virginia, whom we had not seen for fifty years, J. H. Elliot, Charles H. Gates, J. L. Goodridge, E. R. Hoar, W. Ingalls, J. Alsop King (fifty years nearly), A. A. Lawrence, H. Lyon, C. W. Palfrey, Charles H. Parker,

W. R. Robeson, C. C. Shackford, C. W. Storey, F. M. Weld, B. H. West.

"There were living, but not there, W. H. Allen (off West; he wrote a good letter); J. S. Beal (fading out at Kingston); W. F. Frick, Baltimore (he ought to have come); F. Jones; Edward Lander (in Washington); L. Stephens; N. L. White; F. E. White (very ill); Samuel Willard (sick and blind). There was a plenty to eat and drink, all of which was furnished by E. R. Hoar. We were joyous for a while, but sad when we reflected that this is the last meeting on earth for most of us.

"After our meeting in Holworthy, we joined the procession of graduates to Memorial Hall. J. Russell Lowell and others made speeches, Choate of New York presided, Hoar answered for our class. God bless the dear old boys for the remnant of their days."

For two or three years his brother William's health had been failing, and instead of the morning call in Longwood of William upon Amos, and the return call at sunset, there was now only the sunset call. After dusk on the winter evenings, Amos, with imperfect vision, would slowly make his way over the familiar path to William's house; and then the brothers, with one hand on the other's knee, would talk over the little family matters, recount their blessings, and confirm each other in their faith, while an occasional laugh would reveal the fact that behind the feeble voice of the invalid was a witty mind and genial heart.

It was one of the pleasures of Nahant that Mr. Lawrence was within driving distance of his brother, who always passed the summer at Swampscott. But in the summer of 1885 the drives to Swampscott were sad ones; for William was slowly sinking, and was able only at times to " whisper that he had company always, for the angel of the Lord encampeth round about them that fear Him, and delivereth them."

On the 20th of September he peacefully fell asleep, and three days later his body was taken from the memorial church at Longwood to Mount Auburn.

His brother, the last surviving member of his father's family, returned to Waban Farm to write: " Farewell, dear brother, until we meet again in the presence of God and his angels, and of those whom we have loved and who have gone before."

Again followed the routine-calls upon the sick, with the day's text, " Be of good courage, and He shall strengthen your heart ; " sleepless nights after days of depression ; and in spite of rapidly increasing blindness, horseback rides, and activities in many interests. On Thanksgiving Day there was the usual family gathering. " We played games, we older ones joined in them all ; blind man's buff, puss in the corner, ' contra-dance,' etc. My heart was very sad, but I concealed it." With Christmas comes the thought: " There can be but few more Christmas Days for me on earth, for the lights are fading out for me ; my sight has become dim with the eye which remains ; the other sees not at all."

Three weeks later he records : —

" January 18, 1886. My dear wife tells me, before we are up, of the decision to operate on my eye at once. Dr. Derby was here yesterday and advised it. Dr. Hodges came this morning. God my Father give me fortitude to bear it all, and faith in his goodness now and evermore."

The next day the operation took place successfully. Mr. Lawrence met the trial with great calmness, and endured the darkness of several weeks with patience. His first thought, a few minutes after the operation, was to have two checks sent to the Blind Asylum and to an industrial school.

The calls of his many friends and of his children gave him great comfort. And he was particularly happy in the companionship of his friend and classmate, Charles H. Gates, who from this time devoted himself to Mr. Lawrence ; walking, driving, and reading with him.

As soon as he was able to go out, he was so anxious to call upon all those who, during his confinement, had been sick or afflicted, that the strain on his sympathies had to be checked by the doctor. Nevertheless the pen of his wife or of Mr. Gates was set to work on messages of sympathy.

The early summer was passed in visits to his children at their summer places in Beverly, Medford, and Newport, and then came the quiet of Nahant. The days were brightened by increasing clearness of vision, and by the restoration to health of his youngest daughter, who had been three years an invalid and away from home.

Sharp pains across the chest, and an increasing inability to walk, cramped his activity.   His birthday passed with the record:

"Seventy-two.   Sustain me, O God! during what remains to me of life.   Enable me to be still of some use in this world.   Give me courage to live cheerfully and to do my duty, to be helpful to my dear wife, who is so helpful to me, and to my dear children and grand-children."

With a daughter and her family next door, and guests within and friends all about, he followed his routine of life, going to his office in Boston two or three times a week. "This text," he wrote, "has helped me much: 'Let us not be weary in well-doing, for in due season we shall reap if we faint not.'"

On Sunday, August 22, he, his wife, and Mr. Gates formed the family in the house where ten or twelve young people used to sit at table.   The day before, his friends, Dr. and Mrs. Slade, had left after a short visit. In the morning he went to church as usual, when, as he wrote his son later, "the preacher was a bright man, they say. Mr. Beal said his sermon was very powerful. Gates wondered what it was about. I tried hard to admire it and be benefited by it, but think the air must have been poor in the church."

But his heart was heavy with the sad downfall of a friend and neighbor whom he had lately visited in sympathy. He was restless and could think of nothing else; "sad, sad," he wrote and felt that afternoon. However, as usual, he made some calls and then walked home to tea. His son-in-law came in, and again the sad subject was touched upon; soon the last visitor had gone and the house was closed. He went up-stairs to his room, lighted his candle, and then a heavy thud upon the floor warned his wife that he had fallen. Before she could reach him the life had departed; the heart which, through many active years, had beaten so strong in sympathy, was worn out and had ceased to do its work.

Thirty-four years before his father had fallen asleep just as suddenly and as peacefully, and in his journal Mr. Lawrence had then recorded: "May God grant to me as peaceful a release from this body as was granted to him! God of my fathers, help me to live a holy life; help me by my example to lead those who look up to me in the heavenly life."

His prayer was answered in life and death. On the 25th of August, less than a year after his brother's death, the church which they had built was crowded with relatives, friends, and citizens, rich and poor.

The funeral service was read by the Rev. R. H. Howe, the rector of the church, and by Mr. Lawrence's nephew, the Rev. Arthur Lawrence. The body was carried from the church by eight nephews, and was then borne through Cambridge and by Lawrence Hall to Mount Auburn, where it was laid to rest in the Lawrence lot. Over it was placed a stone cut with a text of his own choice: " Be of good courage, and He shall strengthen your heart, all ye that hope in the Lord."

INDEX.